In Harlequin Presents books seduction and passion are
always guaranteed, and this month is no exception!
You'll love what we have to offer you this April....

Favorite author Helen Bianchin brings us
The Marriage Possession, where a devilishly
handsome millionaire demands his pregnant
mistress marry him. In part two of Sharon Kendrick's
enticingly exotic THE DESERT PRINCES trilogy,
The Sheikh's Unwilling Wife, the son of a powerful
desert ruler is determined to make his estranged wife
resume her position by his side.

If you love passionate Mediterranean men, then these
books will definitely be ones to look out for! In
Lynne Graham's *The Italian's Inexperienced Mistress*,
an Italian tycoon finds that one night with an innocent
English girl just isn't enough! Then in Kate Walker's
Sicilian Husband, Blackmailed Bride, a sinfully
gorgeous Sicilian vows to reclaim his wife in his bed.
In *At the Greek Boss's Bidding,* Jane Porter brings you
an arrogant Greek billionaire whose temporary blindness
leads to an intense relationship with his nurse.

And for all of you who want to be whisked away by
a rich man... *The Secret Baby Bargain*
by Melanie Milburne tells the story of a ruthless
multimillionaire returning to take his ex-fiancée
as his wife. In *The Millionaire's Runaway Bride*
by Catherine George, the electric attraction between
a vulnerable PA and her wealthy ex proves
too tempting to resist.

Finally, we have a brand-new author for you!
In Abby Green's *Chosen as the Frenchman's Bride* a tall,
bronzed Frenchman takes an innocent virgin as his wife.
Be sure to look out for more from Abby very soon!

RED HOT REVENGE

There are times in a man's life...

when only seduction will settle old scores!

Pick up our exciting series of revenge-filled romances—they're recommended and red-hot!

Available only from Harlequin Presents®

Melanie Milburne

THE SECRET BABY BARGAIN

RED HOT REVENGE

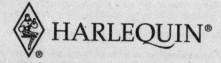

HARLEQUIN®

TORONTO • NEW YORK • LONDON
AMSTERDAM • PARIS • SYDNEY • HAMBURG
STOCKHOLM • ATHENS • TOKYO • MILAN • MADRID
PRAGUE • WARSAW • BUDAPEST • AUCKLAND

If you purchased this book without a cover you should be aware
that this book is stolen property. It was reported as "unsold and
destroyed" to the publisher, and neither the author nor the
publisher has received any payment for this "stripped book."

ISBN-13: 978-0-373-12624-8
ISBN-10:   0-373-12624-7

THE SECRET BABY BARGAIN

First North American Publication 2007.

Copyright © 2006 by Melanie Milburne.

All rights reserved. Except for use in any review, the reproduction or
utilization of this work in whole or in part in any form by any electronic,
mechanical or other means, now known or hereafter invented, including
xerography, photocopying and recording, or in any information storage
or retrieval system, is forbidden without the written permission of the
publisher, Harlequin Enterprises Limited, 225 Duncan Mill Road,
Don Mills, Ontario, Canada M3B 3K9.

All characters in this book have no existence outside the imagination of
the author and have no relation whatsoever to anyone bearing the same
name or names. They are not even distantly inspired by any individual
known or unknown to the author, and all incidents are pure invention.

This edition published by arrangement with Harlequin Books S.A.

® and TM are trademarks of the publisher. Trademarks indicated with
® are registered in the United States Patent and Trademark Office, the
Canadian Trade Marks Office and in other countries.

www.eHarlequin.com

Printed in U.S.A.

All about the author…
Melanie Milburne

MELANIE read her first Harlequin novel when she was seventeen and has never looked back. She decided she would settle for nothing less than a tall, dark and handsome hero as her future husband. Well, she's not only still reading romance, but writing it as well! And as for the tall, dark and handsome hero, she fell in love with him on the second date and was secretly engaged to him within six weeks!

Two sons later, they arrived in Hobart, Tasmania— the jewel in the Australian crown. Once their boys were in school, Melanie went back to university and received her bachelor and then master's degree.

For her final assessment, she conducted a tutorial in literary theory concentrating on the romance genre. As she was reading a paragraph from the novel of a prominent Harlequin author, the door suddenly burst open. The husband that she thought was working was actually standing there dressed in a tuxedo, his dark brown eyes centred on her startled blue ones. He strode across the room, hauled Melanie into his arms and kissed her deeply and passionately before setting her back down and leaving without a single word. The lecturer gave Melanie a high distinction and her fellow students gave her jealous glares! And so her pilgrimage into romance writing was set!

Melanie also enjoys long-distance running and is a nationally ranked top-ten masters swimmer in Australia. She learned to swim as an adult, so for anyone who thinks they can't do something—you can! Her motto is "Don't say I can't; say I CAN TRY."

CHAPTER ONE

ASHLEIGH knew something was wrong as soon as she entered her parents' house on Friday evening after work.

'Mum?' She dropped her bag to the floor, her gaze sweeping the hall for her three-, nearly four-year-old son before turning back to her mother's agitated expression. 'What's going on? Where's Lachlan?'

Gwen Forrester twisted her hands together, her usually cheerful features visibly contorted with strain. 'Darling…' She gave a quick nervous swallow. 'Lachlan is fine… Your father took him fishing a couple of hours ago.'

Ashleigh's frown deepened. 'Then what on earth is the matter? You look as if you've just seen a ghost.'

'I don't quite know how to tell you this…' Gwen took her daughter's hands in hers and gave them a gentle squeeze.

Ashleigh felt her heart begin to thud with alarm. The last time she'd seen her mother this upset had been when she'd returned from London to deliver her bombshell news.

Her heart gave another sickening thump and her breathing came to a stumbling halt. Surely this wasn't about Jake Marriott? Not after all this time… It had been years…four and a half years…

'Mum, come on, you're really freaking me out. Whatever's the matter with you?'

'Ashleigh…he's back.'

Ashleigh felt the cold stream of icy dread begin to flow through her veins, her limbs suddenly freezing and her stomach folding over in panic.

'He called in a short while ago,' Gwen said, her soft blue eyes communicating her concern.

'What?' Ashleigh finally found her voice. *'Here? In person?'*

'Don't worry.' Gwen gave her daughter's hands another reassuring squeeze. 'Lachlan had already left with your father. He didn't see him.'

'But what about the photos?' Ashleigh's stomach gave another savage twist when she thought of the virtual gallery of photographs her parents had set up in the lounge room, each and every one of them documenting their young grandson's life to date. Then, as another thought hit her like a sledgehammer, she gasped, 'Oh, my God, what about his toys?'

'He didn't see anything. I didn't let Jake past the hallway and I'd already done a clean-up after your father left with Lachlan.'

'Thank God…' She slipped out of her mother's hold and sank to the telephone table chair, putting her head in her hands in an attempt to collect her spinning thoughts.

Jake was back!

Four and a half lonely heartbreaking years and he was back in Australia.

Here.

In Sydney.

She lifted her head from her hands and faced her mother once more. 'What did he want?'

'He wants to see you,' Gwen said. 'He wouldn't take no for an answer.'

So that much hadn't changed, she thought cynically. Jake Marriott was a man well used to getting his way and was often unashamedly ruthless in going about it.

'I can't see him.' She sprang to her feet in agitation and began to pace the hall. 'I just can't.'

'Darling…' Her mother's tone held a touch of gentle but unmistakable reproach. 'You really should have told him about Lachlan by now. He has a right to know he fathered a child.'

'He has no right!' Ashleigh turned on her mother in sudden anger. 'He never wanted a child. He made that clear from the word go. No marriage—no kids. That was the deal.'

'All the same, he still should have been informed.'

Ashleigh drew in a scalding breath as the pain of the past assaulted her afresh. 'You don't get it, do you, Mum? Even after all these years you still want to make him out to be the good guy.' She gave her mother an embittered glance and continued, 'Well, for your information, if I had told Jake I was pregnant he would've steamrollered me into having a termination. I just know he would've insisted on it.'

'That choice would have been yours, surely?' Gwen offered, her expression still clouded with motherly concern. 'He could hardly have forced you into it.'

'I was barely twenty years old!' Ashleigh said, perilously close to tears. 'I was living overseas with a man nine years older than me, for whom I would have done anything. If he had told me to jump off the Tower of London I probably would have done it.' She let out a ragged breath. 'I loved him so much…'

Gwen sighed as she took her daughter in her arms, one of her hands stroking the silky ash-blonde head as she had done for almost all of Ashleigh's twenty-four years.

'Oh, Mum…' Ashleigh choked on a sob as she lifted her head. 'What am I going to do?'

Gwen put her from her gently but firmly, her inbuilt pragmatism yet again coming to the fore. 'You will see him because, if nothing else, you owe him that. He mentioned his father has recently passed away. I suppose that's why he's returned to Sydney, to put his father's affairs in order.'

Ashleigh's brow creased in a puzzled little frown as she followed her mother into the kitchen. When she'd asked Jake about his family in the past he'd told her that both his parents were dead. During the time they'd been together he had rarely spoken of his childhood and had deliberately shied away from the topic whenever she'd probed him. She'd put it down to the grief he must have felt at losing both his parents so young.

Why had he lied to her?

'Did he say where he was staying?' she asked as she dragged out one of the breakfast bar stools in the kitchen and sat down.

Gwen busied herself with filling the kettle as she answered. 'At a hotel at the moment, but I got the impression he was moving somewhere here on the North Shore.'

She stared at her mother in shock. 'That close?'

'I'm afraid so,' Gwen said. 'You're going to have a hard time keeping Lachlan's existence a secret if he ends up living in a neighbouring suburb.'

Ashleigh didn't answer but her expression communicated her worry.

'You really have no choice but to see him and get it over with,' Gwen said as she handed her a cup. 'Anyway, for all you know he might have changed.'

Ashleigh bit back a snort of cynicism. 'I don't think people like Jake Marriott ever change. It's not in their nature.'

'You know you can be pretty stubborn yourself at times, Ashleigh,' her mother chided. 'I know you've needed to be strong to be a single mother, but sometimes I think you chop off your nose to spite your face. You should have been well and truly married by now. I don't know why poor Howard puts up with it, really I don't.'

Ashleigh rolled her eyes, gearing herself up for one of her mother's lectures on why she should push the wedding forward a few months. Howard Caule had made it more than clear that he wanted to bring up Lachlan as his own, but every time he'd tried to set a closer date for their wedding she'd baulked. She still wasn't entirely sure why.

'You do love him, don't you, Ashleigh?'

'Who?' She looked at her mother blankly.

'Howard,' Gwen said, her expression shadowed with a little frown. 'Who else?'

Ashleigh wasn't sure how to answer.

She cared for Howard, very deeply, in fact. He'd been a wonderful friend to her—standing by her while she got back on her feet, offering her a part-time position as a buyer for his small chain of antique stores. But as for love… Well, she didn't really trust such volatile feelings any more. It was much safer for her to care for people in an affectionate, friendly but slightly distant manner.

'Howard understands I'm not quite ready for marriage,' she said. 'Anyway, he knows I want to wait until Lachlan settles into his first year at school before I disrupt his life with any further changes to his routine.'

'Are you sleeping with him?'

'*Mum!*' Ashleigh's face flamed with heated colour.

Gwen folded her arms across her chest. 'You've known Howard for over three years. How long did you know Jake before you went to bed with him?'

Ashleigh refused to answer; instead she sent her mother a glowering look.

'Three days, wasn't it?' Gwen asked, ignoring her daughter's fiery glare.

'I've learnt my lesson since then,' Ashleigh bit out.

'Darling, I'm not lecturing you on what's right and wrong.' She gave a deep and expressive sigh. 'I just think you might be better able to handle seeing Jake again if things were a little more permanent in your relationship with Howard. I don't want to see you hurt all over again.'

'I won't allow Jake to hurt me again,' Ashleigh said with much more confidence than she had any hope of feeling. 'I will see him but that's all. I can't possibly tell him about Lachlan.'

'But surely Lachlan has the right to meet his father at some point? If Jake stays in Sydney for any length of time you will have no choice but to tell him of his son's existence. Imagine what he would think if he were to find out some other way.'

'I hate to disillusion you, Mum, but this is one thing Jake will never budge on. He would be absolutely furious to find out he had a son. I just know it. It was one of the things we argued about the most.' She bit her lip as the memory of their bitter parting scored her brutally, before she continued. 'He would be so angry…so terribly angry…'

Gwen reached into her pocket and handed Ashleigh a card. 'He left this card so you can contact him. He's staying at a hotel in the city. He apparently wants some work done on his father's house before he moves in. I think it would be wise to see him on neutral territory.'

Ashleigh looked down at the card in her hand, her stomach clenching painfully as she saw his name printed there in silver writing.

Jake Marriott CEO Marriott Architecture.

She lifted her gaze back to her mother, resignation heavy in her tone. 'Will you and Dad be all right with minding Lachlan if I go now?'

Gwen gave her a soft smile. 'That's my girl. Go and get it over with, then you can get on with your life knowing you did the right thing in the end.'

Ashleigh stood outside the plush city hotel half an hour later and wondered if she was even in her right mind, let alone doing the right thing. She hadn't rung the mobile number printed on Jake's business card to inform him of her intention to see him. She told herself it was because she didn't want him to have the advantage of preparing himself for her arrival, but deep down she knew it had more to do with her own cowardice.

In the end she had to wait for him, because the reception desk attendant refused to give Jake's room number without authorisation from him first.

She decided against sitting on one of the comfortable-looking leather sofas in the piano lounge area and took a stool at the bar instead, perching on the edge of it with a glass of soda water in her hand, which she knew she'd never be able to swallow past the lump of dread blocking her throat.

As if she could sense his arrival, she found her gaze tracking towards the bank of lifts, his tall unmistakable figure stepping out of the far right one, every scrap of air going out of her lungs as he came into full view.

She knew she was staring at him but just couldn't help it. In four and a half years he had not changed other than to look even more devastatingly handsome.

His imposing height gave him a proud, almost aristocratic bearing and his long lean limbs displayed the physical evidence of his continued passion for endurance sports. His clothes hung on his frame with lazy grace; he had never been the designer type but whatever he wore managed to look top of the range regardless. His wavy black hair was neither long nor short but brushed back in a careless manner which could have indicated the recent use of a hairbrush; however she thought it was more likely to have been the rake of his long tanned fingers that had achieved that just-out-of-bed look.

She was surprised at how painful it was to look at him again.

She'd known every nuance of his face, her fingers had traced over every hard contour of his body, her gentle touch lingering over the inch-long scar above his right eyebrow, her lips kissing him in every intimate place, and yet as he strode towards her she felt as if she had never known him at all.

He had simply not allowed her to.

'Hello, Ashleigh.'

Ashleigh had trouble disguising her reaction to his deep voice, the smooth velvet tones with just a hint of an English accent woven through it. How she had longed to hear it over the years!

'Hello.' She met his dark eyes briefly, hoping he wouldn't see the guilt reflected in hers at the thought of what she had kept hidden from him for all this time.

'You're looking well,' Jake said, his gaze running over her in a sweeping but all-encompassing glance. 'Have you put on weight?'

Ashleigh pursed her lips for a moment before responding with a touch of tartness. 'I see your idea of what constitutes a compliment is still rather twisted.'

One eyebrow rose and his mouth lifted in a small mocking smile. 'I see you're still as touchy as ever.' His eyes dipped to her breasts for a moment before returning slowly to hers. 'I think it suits you. You were always so bone-thin.'

'It must have been the stress of living with you,' she shot back before she could stop herself, reaching for her drink with an unsteady hand.

A tight little silence fell in the space between them.

Ashleigh felt like kicking herself for betraying her bitterness so unguardedly. She stared at a floating ice cube in her glass, wishing she was able to see Jake without it doing permanent damage to her emotional well-being.

'You're probably right,' Jake said, a tiny frown settling between his brows and, as he took the stool beside her, lifted his hand to get the barman's attention.

Ashleigh swivelled on her stool to stare at him. Was that regret she could hear in his tone?

She waited until he'd given the barman his order and his drink had arrived before speaking again.

'My mother told me why you're here.'

His gaze met hers but he didn't answer. Something indefinable flickered in the depths of his coal-black eyes before he turned back to his drink and took a deep draught.

Ashleigh watched the up and down movement of his throat as he swallowed. He was sitting so close she could touch him but it felt as if there was an invisible wall around him.

'Why did you tell me when we met that both your parents were dead?' she asked when she could stand the silence no longer.

'It seemed the easiest thing to say at the time.'

'Yes, well, lying was always something that came very naturally to you,' she bit out resentfully.

He turned to look at her, his darker-than-night eyes holding hers. 'It might surprise you to hear this, but I didn't like lying to you, Ashleigh. I just thought it was less complicated than explaining everything.'

Ashleigh stared at him as he took another sip of his drink, her heart feeling too tight, as if the space allocated for it had suddenly been drastically reduced. What did he mean—'explain everything'?

She let another silence pass before she asked, 'When did you arrive?'

'A couple of weeks ago. I thought I'd wait until after the funeral to see if he left me anything in his will.' He drained his glass and set it back down with a nerve-jangling crack on the bar in front of him.

There was a trace of something in his voice that suggested he hadn't been all that certain of his father's intentions regarding his estate. Ashleigh was surprised at how tempted she was to reach out and touch him, to offer him some sort of comfort for what he was going through. She had to hold on to her glass with both hands to stop herself from doing so, knowing he wouldn't welcome it in the bitter context of their past relationship.

'And did he?' She met his eyes once more. 'Leave you anything?'

A cynical half smile twisted his mouth as his eyes meshed with hers. 'He left me everything he didn't want for himself.'

She had to look away from the burning heat of his eyes. She stared down at the slice of lemon in her glass. 'It must be very hard for you…just now.'

Jake gave an inward grimace as he watched her toy with her straw, her small neat fingers demonstrating her unease in his company.

The hardest thing he'd ever had to do was to look her up that afternoon. His pride, his damned pride, had insisted he was a fool for doing so, but in the end he'd overridden it for just one look at her.

When he'd seen her mother at the house he'd considered waiting for however long it took for Ashleigh to return, but sensing Mrs Forrester's discomfiture had reluctantly left. He hadn't been entirely sure she would have even told Ashleigh of his call. He could hardly blame her, of course. No doubt Ashleigh had told her family what a pig-headed selfish bastard he'd been to her all the time they'd been together.

But he *had* to see her.

He had to see her to remind himself of what he'd thrown away.

'Yes…it's not been easy,' he admitted, staring into his empty glass.

He felt her shift beside him and had to stop himself from turning to her and hauling her into his arms.

She looked fantastic.

She'd grown into her body in a way few women these days did. Her figure had pleased him no end in the past, but now it was riper, more womanly, her softer curves making him ache to mould her to him as he had done in the past.

If only they had just met now, without the spectre of their previous relationship dividing them. But it wasn't *their* past that had divided them—it had been his. And it was only now that he was finally coming to terms with it.

'Your mother looks the same,' he said, sending her another quick glance, taking in her ringless fingers with immeasurable relief.

'Yes…'

'How is your father?'

'Retired now,' Ashleigh answered. 'Enjoying being able to play with…er…'

Jake swung his gaze back to hers at her sudden vocal stall. 'Golf?'

Ashleigh clutched at the sudden lifeline with relief. 'Yes… golf. He plays a lot of golf.'

'I always liked your dad,' he said, looking back at his empty glass again.

The undisguised warmth in his statement moved her very deeply. Ashleigh's family had come over to London for Christmas the second year she'd been living with Jake, and she had watched how Jake had done his best to fit in with her family. When he hadn't been hiding away at work he'd spent a bit of time with her father, choosing his company instead of the boisterous and giggling presence of her younger sisters, Mia and Ellie, and her trying-too-hard mother. She had been touched by his effort to include himself in her family's activities, his tall, somewhat aloof, presence often seeming out of place and awkward amidst the rough and tumble of the family interactions that she had always taken for granted.

'How are your sisters?' he asked after another little pause.

A small smile of pride flickered on her mouth. 'Mia is trying her best to get into acting, with some limited success.

She was a pot plant in a musical a month ago; we were all incredibly proud of her. And Ellie… Well, you know Ellie.' Her expression softened at the thought of her adopted youngest sister. 'She is still the world's biggest champion for the underdog. She works part-time in a café and spends every other available minute at a dogs' home as a volunteer.'

'And what about you?' Jake asked, looking at her intently.

'Me?' She gave him a startled look, her pulses racing at the intensity of his dark eyes as they rested on her face. His smile had softened his normally harsh features, the simple upward movement of his lips unleashing a flood of memories about how that mouth had felt on hers…

'Yes, you,' he said. 'What are you doing with yourself these days?'

'I…' She swallowed and tried to appear unfazed by his question. 'Not much.' She twirled her straw a couple of times and continued. 'I work as a buyer for an antique dealer.' She pushed her glass away and met his eyes again. 'Howard Caule Antiques.'

He gestured to the barman to refresh their drinks, taking his time to turn back to her to respond. 'I've heard of him.' He picked up his glass as soon as it was placed in front of him. 'What's he like to work for?'

For some reason Ashleigh found it difficult to meet his eyes with any equanimity. She moistened her lips, her stomach doing a funny little somersault when she saw the way his eyes followed the nervous movement of her tongue.

'He's…he's nice.'

Damn it! She chided herself as she saw the way Jake's lip instantly curled. Why couldn't she have thought of a better adjective than that?

'A nice guy, huh?'

She had to look away. 'Yes. He's also one of my closest friends.'

'Are you sleeping with him?'

Her eyes flew back to his, her cheeks flaming for the second time that day. 'That's absolutely no business of yours.'

He didn't respond immediately, which made her tension go up another excruciating notch. She watched him as he surveyed her with those dark unreadable eyes, every nerve in her body jumping in sharp awareness at his proximity.

She could even *smell* him.

Her nostrils flared to take in more of that evocative scent, the combination of full-blooded-late-in-the-day active male and his particular choice of aftershave that had always reminded her of sun-warmed lemons and exotic spices.

'My my my, you are touchy, aren't you?' he asked, the mocking smile still in place.

She set her mouth and turned to stare at the full glass in front of her, wishing herself a million miles away.

She couldn't do this.

She couldn't be calm and cool in Jake Marriott's presence. He unsettled her in every way possible.

'I'm not being touchy.' Her tone was brittle and on edge. 'I just don't see what my private life has to do with you...*now*.'

His continued silence drew her gaze back as if he'd pulled it towards him with invisible strings.

'Ashleigh...' He reached out to graze her cheek with the back of his knuckles in a touch so gentle she felt a great wave of emotion swamp her for what they'd had and subsequently lost.

She fought her feelings down with an effort, her teeth tearing at the inside of her mouth as she held his unwavering gaze.

'I'd like to see you again while I'm here in Sydney,' he said, his deep voice sounding ragged and uneven. 'I'm here for a few weeks and I thought we could—' he deliberately paused over the words '—catch up.'

Ashleigh inwardly seethed. She could just imagine what he meant by catching up; a bit of casual sex to fill in the time before he left the country to go back to whoever was waiting for him back in London.

'I can't see you.'

His eyes hardened momentarily and his hand fell away. 'Why not?'

She bit her lip, hunting her brain for the right words to describe her relationship with Howard.

'Is there someone else?' he asked before she could respond, his eyes dipping to her bare fingers once more.

She drew in a tight breath. 'Yes…yes there is.'

'You're not wearing a ring.'

She gave him an ironic look and clipped back, 'I lived and slept with you for two whole years without needing one.'

Jake shifted slightly as he considered her pert response. Her cheeks were bright with colour, her eyes flashing him a warning he had no intention of heeding.

He knew it bordered on the arrogant to assume that no one had taken his place after four and a half years, but he'd hoped for it all the same. His own copybook wasn't too pristine, of course; he'd replaced her numerous times, but not one of his subsequent lovers had affected him the way Ashleigh had, and, God help him, still did.

'What would you say if I told you I've had a rethink of a few of my old standpoints?' he asked. 'That I'd changed?'

Ashleigh got to her feet and, rummaging in her purse, placed some money on the counter for her drink, her eyes when they returned to his like twin points of angry blue flame.

'I'd say you were four and a half years too late, Jake Marriott.' She hoisted her bag back on her shoulder. 'I have to go. I have someone waiting for me.'

She turned to leave but one of his hands came down on

her wrist and turned her round to face him. She felt the velvet-covered steel bracelet of his fingers and suppressed an inward shiver of reaction at feeling his warm flesh on hers once more.

'Let me go, Jake.' Her voice came out husky instead of determined, making her hate him for affecting her so.

He rose to his full height, his body within a whisper of hers. She felt as if she couldn't breathe, for if she so much as drew in one small breath her chest would expand and bring her breasts into contact with the hard wall of his chest. Dark eyes locked with blue in a battle she knew she was never going to win, but she had to fight regardless.

'I can't see you, Jake,' she said in a tight voice. 'I am engaged to be married.' She took another shaky breath and added, 'To my boss, Howard Caule.'

She saw the sudden flare of heat in his eyes at the same time the pressure of his fingers subtly increased about her wrist.

'You're not married yet,' he said, before dropping her wrist and stepping back from her.

Ashleigh wasn't sure if his statement was a threat or an observation. She didn't stay around to find out. Instead, she turned on her heel and stalked out of the bar with long purposeful strides that she hoped gave no hint of her inner distress.

Jake watched her go, his chest feeling as if some giant hand had just plunged between his ribs and wrenched out his heart and slapped it down on the bar next to the ten dollar note she'd placed beside her untouched drink...

CHAPTER TWO

ASHLEIGH drove back to her parents' house with her bottom lip between her teeth for the entire journey.

It had *hurt* to see Jake again.

It had *hurt* her to hear his voice, to see his hands grip his glass—the hands that had once caressed her and with his very male body brought her to the highest pinnacle of human pleasure.

It had *hurt* to see his mouth tilt in a smile—the mouth that had kissed her all over but had never once spoken of his love.

Damn it! It had *hurt* to turn him down, but what other choice did she have? She could hardly pick up where they'd left off. How could she, with the secret of Lachlan's existence lying between them? Jake had made it clear he never wanted to have children. She could hardly tap him on the shoulder and announce, *By the way, here is your son. Don't you think he looks a bit like you?*

'Mummee!' Lachlan rushed towards her as soon as she opened the door, throwing his little arms around her middle and squeezing tightly.

'Hey, why aren't you in bed?' She pretended to frown down at him.

His chocolate-brown eyes twinkled as he looked up at her.

'Grandad promised me I could show you what we caught first.'

She looked up at her father, who had followed his young grandson out into the hall. 'Hi, Dad. Good day at the bay?'

Heath Forrester grinned. 'You should have seen the ones we let get away.'

Ashleigh smiled and stood on tiptoe to plant a soft kiss on his raspy cheek. 'Thanks,' she said, her one word speaking a hundred for her.

Heath turned to Lachlan. 'Go and get our bounty out of the fridge while I have a quick word with your mum.'

Lachlan raced off, the sound of his footsteps echoing down the hall as Heath turned to his eldest daughter. 'How was Jake?'

'He was…' she let out a little betraying sigh '…Jake.'

'What did he want?'

'I got the distinct impression he wanted to resume our past relationship—temporarily.'

Her father's bushy brows rose slightly. 'Same old Jake then?'

She gave him a world-weary sigh. 'Same old Jake.'

'You didn't tell him about Lachlan?'

Ashleigh hunted her father's expression for the reproach she privately dreaded, but found none and was immensely grateful for it.

'No…' She inspected her hands for a moment. 'No, I didn't.'

'Howard called while you were out.' Heath changed the subject tactfully. 'He said something about taking you out to dinner. I told him you'd call but if you want me to put him off I can always—'

Ashleigh forced her mouth into a smile and tucked her arm through one of his. 'Why don't we go and look at that fish first?'

'What a good idea,' he said and led her towards the kitchen.

An hour later Lachlan was fast asleep upstairs and Ashleigh made her way downstairs again, only to be halted by her

sister Mia who had not long come in from an actors and per-
formers' workshop.

'Is it true?' Mia ushered her into the study, out of the hearing of the rest of the Forrester family. 'Is Jake really back in
Sydney?'

Ashleigh gave a single nod. 'Yes…he's back.'

Mia let out a very unladylike phrase. 'Have you told him
about Lachlan?' she asked.

Ashleigh shook her head. 'No…'

Mia's eyes widened. 'What are you doing? Of course he
has to know now that he's back.'

'Listen, Mia. I've already had this sort of lecture from
Mum, so I don't need another one from you.'

Mia held up her hands in a gesture of surrender. 'Hey,
don't get all shirty with me, but have you actually listened to
that kid of yours lately? All he ever talks about is dad stuff.'

Ashleigh frowned. 'What do you mean?'

Mia gave her a sobering look. 'I read him a story the other
night when you were out with Howard. You know, the one
about the elephant with the broken trunk who was looking
for someone to fix it? Lachlan kept on and on about how if
he could find his real dad he was sure he would be able to fix
everything. How cute, but how sad, is that?'

Ashleigh turned away, her hands clenching in tension. 'I
can't deal with this right now. I have enough to think about
without you adding to it.'

'Come on, Ash,' Mia said. 'What's to think about? Jake
has come home to Sydney and he should be told the truth.
It's not like you can hide it from him. One close look at that
kid and he's going to see it for himself.'

Ashleigh felt the full force of her sister's words like a blow
to her mid-section. Lachlan was the spitting image of his
father. His darker-than-night eyes, his long rangy limbs, his
black hair that refused to stay in place, his temper that could

rise and fall with the weight of a timely smile or gentle caress…

The doorbell sounded and Ashleigh turned and walked down the hall to answer it rather than continue the conversation with her sister.

'Ashleigh,' Howard Caule greeted her warmly, pressing a quick kiss to her cheek as he came in. 'How's my girl?' He caught sight of Mia hovering. 'Hi, Mia, how are the auditions for the toilet paper advertisement going?'

'Great, I'm going to wipe the floor with the competition,' Mia answered with an insincere smile and a roll of her eyes before she walked away.

Ashleigh dampened down her annoyance at her sister's behaviour towards her fiancé, knowing it would be pointless to try and defend him. Mia and Ellie had never taken to him no matter how many times she highlighted his good points. It caused her a great deal of pain but there was nothing she could do about it. Howard was reliable and safe and more or less wanted the same things in life that she did. Her family would just have to get used to the idea of him being a permanent fixture in her life. Lachlan liked him and as far as she was concerned that counted for more than anything.

Once Mia had gone she closed the front door and leant back against it, her eyes going to Howard's. 'We have to talk.'

'Let's do it over dinner,' he suggested. Then, taking something out of his pocket, he added, 'Is Lachlan still awake? I brought him a little present.'

Ashleigh took the toy car he held out to her, her expression softening with gratitude. 'He's asleep but I'll leave it on his bedside table for him. Thank you; you're so good to him.'

'He's a good kid, Ashleigh,' he said. 'I can't wait until we're finally married so I can be a real father to him.'

She gave him a weak smile. 'I'll just tell my folks we're leaving.'

'I'll go and start the car,' he offered helpfully and bounded back out the front door.

Ashleigh spoke briefly with her parents before joining Howard in his car, all the time trying to think of a way to bring up the subject of Jake Marriott.

She had told Howard the barest details of her affair with Lachlan's father, preferring to keep that part of her life separate and distant from the here and now. She hadn't even once mentioned Jake's name. Howard hadn't pressed her, and in a way that was why she valued his friendship so much. He seemed to sense her pain in speaking of the past and always kept things on an upbeat keel to lift her spirits.

Howard was so different from Jake, and not just physically, although those differences were as marked as could ever be. Howard had the typically pale freckled skin that was common to most redheads, his height average and his figure tending towards stocky.

Jake's darkly handsome features combined with his imposing height and naturally athletic build were made all the more commanding by his somewhat aloof and brooding personality.

Howard, on the other hand, was uncomplicated. Mia and Ellie described him as boring but Ashleigh preferred to think of him as predictable.

She *liked* predictable.

She could handle predictable.

She liked knowing what to expect each day when she turned up to work. Howard was always cheerful and positive, nothing was too much trouble and even if it was he didn't let on but simply got on with the task without complaining.

She wished she was in love with him.

Truly in love.

He was worthy of so much more than she could give him but her experience with Jake had taught her the danger of loving too much and too deeply.

'You're very quiet.' Howard glanced her way as he pulled up at a set of traffic lights.

'Sorry…' She shifted her mouth into a semblance of a smile. 'I've got a lot on my mind.'

He reached over and patted her hand, his freckled fingers cool, nothing like the scorching heat of Jake's when he'd touched her earlier.

Her wrist still felt as if it had been burnt. She looked down at it to see if there were any marks but her creamy skin was surprisingly unblemished.

What a pity her heart hadn't been as lucky.

The restaurant he'd chosen was heavily booked and even though Howard had made a reservation they still had to wait for over half an hour for their table.

As Ashleigh sat with him at the bar she couldn't help thinking how different it would have been if it had been Jake with her. There was no way he would have sat patiently waiting for a table he'd pre-booked. He would have demanded the service he was paying for and, what was more, he would have got it.

'What did you want to talk to me about?' Howard asked as he reached for his mineral water.

Ashleigh took a steadying breath and met his light blue eyes. 'I met with Lachlan's father today.'

He gave her a worried look. 'Does he want to see him?'

'I didn't get around to telling him about Lachlan,' she answered. 'We talked about…other things.'

Howard put his glass down. 'You mean he still doesn't know anything about him? Nothing at all?'

'I know it seems wrong not to tell him, but at the time it was the right decision…and now…well…'

'What about now?' Howard asked. 'Shouldn't he be told at some point?'

Ashleigh had thought of nothing else, especially after what Mia had told her about Lachlan. It seemed wrong that her tiny son could never openly acknowledge his father. And yet after seeing Jake again it brought it home to her just what he had missed in knowing nothing of his son's existence. He had not been there for any of the milestones of Lachlan's life. His first smile, his first words and his very first 'I love you'. Jake had missed out on so much and those years could never be returned to him. But she had done what she had thought was right… She still thought it was right. But somehow…

'Lachlan's father hasn't changed a bit.' She gave a deep regretful sigh. 'I was young, far too young to even be in a relationship let alone with someone as intense as him. I lost myself when I was with him. I forgot how to stand up for myself, for what I believed in. I let him take control… It was a mistake… Our relationship was a mistake.'

'Did you tell him about us?' he asked. 'That we're engaged to be married?'

'Yes…'

He frowned as he looked at her bare hands. 'I wish you'd wear my mother's ring. I know you don't like the design but we could get it altered.'

Ashleigh wished she liked it, too. She wished she liked his mother as well, but nothing in life was perfect and she had learned the hard way to make the most of what was on offer and get on with it.

'I'll think about it,' she said. 'Anyway, it's only a symbol. It means nothing.' The words were not her own but some that Jake had used in the past but she didn't think Howard would appreciate that little detail.

'Come on, let's have dinner and forget all about Lachlan's

father for the rest of tonight,' Howard said as the waiter indicated for them to follow him to their table.

Ashleigh gave him a wan smile as she made her way with him to their seats, but even hours later when she was lying in her bed, willing herself to sleep, she still had not been able to drive all thought of Jake from her mind.

He was there.

Permanently.

His dark disturbing presence reminding her of all that had brought them together and what, in the end, had torn them apart.

Ashleigh had not long arrived at the main outlet of Howard Caule Antiques in Woollahra the next morning when Howard rushed towards her excitedly.

'Ashleigh, I have the most exciting news.'

'What?' She put her bag and sunglasses on the walnut desk before tilting her cheek for his customary kiss. 'Let me guess…you've won the lottery?'

His light blue eyes positively gleamed with excitement. 'No, but it sure feels like it. I have just spoken to a man who has recently inherited a veritable warehouse full of antiques. He wants to sell them all—to us! Can you believe it?' He rubbed his hands together in glee. 'Some of the stuff is priceless, Ashleigh. And he wants us to have it all and he's not even worried about how much we are prepared to pay for it.'

Ashleigh gave a small frown. 'There must be some sort of catch. Why would anyone sell off such valuable pieces to one dealer when he could play the market a bit and get top dollar?'

Howard shrugged one shoulder. 'I don't know, but who cares? You know how worried I've been about how things have been a bit tight lately and this is just the sort of boost I need right now.' He reached for a sheet of paper on his desk and handed it to her. 'I've made an appointment for you to meet with him later this morning at this address.'

'But why me?' she asked, glancing down at the paper, her heart missing a beat when she saw the name printed there.

Jake Marriott.

She lifted her tortured gaze to Howard's blissful one. 'I— I can't do this.' The paper crinkled in her tightening fingers.

'What are you doing?' Howard plucked the crumpled paper out of her hand and began straightening it as if it were a piece of priceless parchment. 'He particularly asked for you,' he said. 'He said he knew your family. I checked him out on a few details. I wouldn't allow you to deal with anyone who I thought was unsafe. He knew both your parents' names and—'

'That's because he's Lachlan's father,' she said bluntly.

Howard's eyes bulged. *'Jake Marriott is Lachlan's father?'*

She gave a single nod, her lips tightly compressed.

'Jake Marriott?' His throat convulsed. 'Jake Marriott as in the billionaire architect who's designed some of the most prestigious buildings around the globe?'

'That's the one,' she said.

'Oh, no…' Howard flopped into the nearest chair, the freckles on his face standing out against the pallor of his shocked face.

Ashleigh gnawed her bottom lip, fear turning her insides to liquid.

Howard sprang back to his feet. 'Well, for one thing, you can't possibly tell him about Lachlan,' he insisted, 'or at least not right now. If you do he'll withdraw the offer. I need this deal, Ashleigh.'

'I'll have to tell him sometime…' She let out a painful breath. 'Mia told me Lachlan has been asking about his father. He must have heard the other kids at crèche talking about their dads. I knew he would eventually want to know but I didn't expect it to be this soon.'

'Let's get married as quickly as possible,' he said, taking

both her hands in his. 'That way Lachlan can start calling me his dad.'

She eased herself out of his hold, suddenly unable to maintain eye contact. 'I don't want to get married yet. I'm not ready.'

'Are you ever going to be ready?' His tone held a trace of bitterness she'd never heard in it before.

She turned back to him, her expression wavering with uncertainty. 'It's such a big step. We haven't even…you know…' Her hands fluttered back to her sides, her face hot with embarrassment.

'I told you I don't believe in sex before marriage,' he said. 'I know it's old-fashioned, but my faith is important to me and I think it's a small sacrifice to make to show my loyalty to you and to God.'

Ashleigh couldn't help wondering what Jake would think of Howard's moral uprightness. Jake hadn't even believed in the sanctity of marriage, much less waiting a decent period before committing himself to a physical relationship. He'd had her in his bed within three days of meeting her and if it hadn't been for the prod of her conscience at the time, she knew he would have succeeded on the very first.

She was trapped by circumstances beyond her control and it terrified her. No matter how much she wished her past would go away and never come back she had a permanent living reminder in her little son. Even now Lachlan was a miniature of his biological father and even if a hundred Howards offered to step into his place no one could ever be the man Lachlan most needed.

Besides, she'd seen this played out before in her adopted sister Ellie's life. Ellie pretended to be unconcerned about who her biological parents were but Ashleigh knew how she secretly longed to find out why she had been relinquished when only a few days old. It didn't matter how loving her adoptive parents and she and Mia as her sisters were, Ellie was like a lost soul looking for a connection she both dreaded and desired.

She took the paper out of Howard's hand with dogged resignation. 'All right, I'll do it. I'll buy the goods from him and keep quiet, but I can't help feeling this could backfire on me.'

'Think about the money,' he said. 'This will take me to the top of the antiques market in Sydney.' He reached for the telephone. 'I have to ring my mother. This has been her dream ever since my father died.'

Ashleigh gave an inward sigh and picked up her bag and sunglasses from the desk. Jake had her in the palm of his hand and she could already feel the press of his fingers as they began to close in on her...

The drive to the address in the leafy northern suburb of Lindfield seemed all too short to Ashleigh in spite of the slow crawl of traffic on the Pacific Highway.

She kept glancing at the clock on the dashboard, the minutes ticking by, increasing her panic second by painful second.

The street she turned into as indicated on the paper Howard had given her was typical of the upper north shore, leafy private gardens shielding imposing homes, speaking quietly but unmistakably of very comfortable wealth.

She pulled up in front of the number of the house she'd been given but there was no sign of Jake. The driveway was empty, the scallop-edged blinds at the windows of the house pulled down low just like lashes over closed eyes.

The front garden was huge and looked a bit neglected, as if no one had bothered to tend it recently, the lawn still green but interspersed with dandelion heads, the soft little clouds of seeds looking as if the slightest breath of wind would disturb their spherical perfection for ever.

She walked up the pathway towards the front door, breathing in the scent of sun-warmed roses as she reached to press the tarnished brass bell.

There was no answer.

She didn't know whether to be relieved or annoyed. According to the information Howard had given her, she was to meet Jake here at eleven a.m. and here it was twelve minutes past and no sign of him.

Typical, she thought as she stepped away from the door. When had Jake ever been the punctual type?

She made her way around to the back of the house, curiosity finally getting the better of her. She wondered if this was the house where he had grown up. He had always been so vague about his childhood but she seemed to remember him mentioning a big garden with an elm tree in the backyard that he used to sometimes climb.

She found it along the tall back fence, its craggy limbs spreading long fingers of shade all over the rear corner of the massive garden. She stepped beneath its dappled shade and looked upwards, trying to picture Jake as a young child scrambling up those ancient limbs to get to the top. He wasn't the bottom branches type, a quality she could already see developing in her little son.

'I used to have a tree-house way up there,' Jake's deep voice said from just behind her.

Ashleigh spun around so quickly she felt light-headed, one of her hands going over her heart where she could feel it leaping towards her throat in shock. 'Y-you scared me!'

He gave her one of his lazy half smiles. 'Did I?'

He didn't seem too bothered about it, she noted with considerable resentment. His expression held a faint trace of amusement as his eyes took in her flustered form.

'You're late,' she said and stepped out of the intimacy of the overhanging branches to the brighter sunlight near a bed of blood-red roses.

'I know,' he answered without apology. 'I had a few things to see to first.'

She tightened her lips and folded her arms across her chest crossly. 'I suppose you think I've got nothing better to do all day than hang around waiting for you to show up. Why didn't you tell me yesterday about this arrangement?'

He joined her next to the roses, stopping for a moment to pick one perfect bloom and, holding it up to his nose, slowly drew in the fragrance.

Ashleigh found it impossible to look away.

The softness of the rose in his large, very male, hand had her instantly recalling his touch on her skin in the past, the velvet-covered steel of his fingers which could stroke like a feather in foreplay, or grasp like a vice in the throes of out of control passion.

She gave an inward shiver as his eyes moved back to meet hers.

He silently handed her the rose and, for some reason she couldn't entirely fathom at the time, she took it from him. She lowered her gaze from his and breathed in the heady scent, feeling the brush of the soft petals against her nose where his had so recently been.

'I'm glad you came,' he said after a little silence. 'I've always wanted you to see where I grew up.'

Ashleigh looked up at him, the rose still in her hand. 'Why?'

He shifted his gaze from hers and sent it to sweep across the garden before turning to look at the house. She watched the movement of his dark unfathomable eyes and couldn't help feeling intrigued by his sudden need to show her the previously private details of his childhood.

It didn't make any sense.

Why now?

Why had it taken him so long to finally reveal things she'd longed to know way back? She had asked him so many times for anecdotes of his childhood but he had skirted around the subject, even shutting her out for days with one of his stony silences whenever she'd prodded him too much.

His eyes came back to hers. 'I used to really hate this place.'

She felt a small frown tug at her forehead. 'Why?'

He seemed to give himself a mental shake, for he suddenly removed his line of vision from hers and began to lead the way towards the house. Ashleigh followed silently, stepping over the cracks in the pathway, wondering what had led him home if it was so painful to revisit this place.

There was so much she didn't know about Jake.

She knew how he took his tea and coffee, she knew he had a terrible sweet tooth attack at about four o'clock every afternoon, she knew he loved his back rubbed and that he had one very ticklish hip. But she didn't know what made his eyes and face become almost mask-like whenever his childhood was mentioned.

Jake unlocked the back door and, leaving Ashleigh hovering in the background, immediately began rolling up blinds and opening windows to let the stale, musty air out.

Ashleigh wasn't sure if she should offer to help or not. She was supposed to be here in a professional capacity but nothing so far in Jake's manner or mood had indicated anything at all businesslike.

'I'm sorry it's so stuffy in here,' he said, stepping past her to reach for the last blind. 'I haven't been here since…well…' He gave her a wry look. 'I haven't been here since I was about sixteen.'

She knew her face was showing every sign of her intrigue but she just couldn't help it. She looked around at the sun-room they were in, but apart from a few uncomfortable-looking chairs and a small table and a cheap self-assembly magazine rack there was nothing that she could see of any great value.

'I know what you're thinking,' he said into the awkward silence.

She looked at him without responding but her eyes obviously communicated her scepticism.

'You're thinking I've led you here on a fool's errand, aren't you?' he asked.

She drew in a small breath and scanned the room once more. 'The contents of this room would barely pay for a cup of coffee and a sandwich at a decent café.' She met his eyes challengingly. 'What's this about, Jake? Why am I here and why now?'

'Come this way.'

He led her towards a door off the sun-room which, when he opened it, showed her a long dark, almost menacing, hallway, the lurking shadows seeming to leap out from the walls to brush at the bare skin of her arms as she followed him about halfway down to a door on the left.

The door opened with a creak of a hinge that protested at the sudden movement, the inner darkness of the room spilling out towards her. Jake flicked on a light switch as she stepped into the room with him, her eyes instantly widening as she saw what was contained within.

She sucked in a breath of wonder as her nostrils filled with the scent of old cedar. The room was stacked almost to the ceiling with priceless pieces of furniture. Tables, chairs, escritoires, chaise longues and bookcases and display cabinets, their dusty shelves filled with an array of porcelain figurines which she instinctively knew were beyond her level of expertise to value with any sort of accuracy. It would take days, if not weeks, to assess the value of each and every item.

She did her best to control her breathing as she stepped towards the first piece of polished cedar, her fingers running over the delicately carved edge as if in worship.

'What do you think?' Jake asked.

She turned to look at him, her hand falling away from the priceless heirloom. 'I think you've picked the wrong person to assess the value of all of this.' She chewed her lip for a moment before adding, 'Howard would be much better able to give you the right—'

'But I want you.'

There was something in his tone that suggested to Ashleigh he wasn't just talking about the furniture.

'I'm not able to help you…' She made to brush past him, suddenly desperate to get out of this house and away from his disturbing presence.

'Wait.' His hand came down on her arm and held her still, leaving her no choice but to meet his dark brooding gaze. 'Don't go.'

She dragged in a ragged breath, her head telling her to get the hell out while she still could, but somehow her treacherous heart insisted she stay.

'Jake…' Her voice sounded as if it had come through a vacuum, it didn't sound at all like her own.

His hand cupped her cheek, his thumb moving over the curve of her lips in a caress so poignantly tender she immediately felt the springing of tears in her eyes.

She watched as his mouth came down towards hers and, in spite of her inner convictions, did absolutely nothing to stop it.

She couldn't.

Her body felt frozen in time, her lips waiting for the imprint of his after four and a half years of deprivation. Her skin begged for his touch with goose-bumps of anticipation springing out all over her, her legs weakening with need as soon as his mouth met hers.

Heat coursed through her at that first blistering touch, her lips instantly swelling under the insistent pressure of his, her mouth opening to the command of his determined tongue as it sought her inner warmth.

She felt the sag of her knees as he crushed her close to his hard frame, the ridges of his body fitting so neatly into the soft curves of hers as if made to measure.

Desire surged through her as if sent on an electric circuit from his. She felt its charge from breast to hip, her body singing with awareness as his body leapt in response against her. She felt the hardening of his growing erection, the heat and length of him a heady, intoxicating reminder of all the intimacies they had shared in the past.

Her body was no mystery to him. He had known every crease and tender fold, had explored and tasted every delicacy with relish. Her body remembered with a desperate burning plea for more. She ached for him, inside and out, her emotions caught up in a maelstrom of feeling she had no control over. It was as if the past hadn't happened; she was his just as she had been all those years ago. He had only to look at her and she would melt into his arms and become whatever he wanted her to become...

She jerked herself out of his hold with a strength she had not known she was capable of and, thankfully for her, he was totally unprepared for.

'You have no right.' She clipped the words out past stiff lips. 'I'm engaged. You have no right to touch me.'

His eyes raked her mercilessly, his expression hinting at satire. 'You gave me the right as soon as you looked at me that way.'

'What way?' She glared at him defensively. 'I did not *look* at you in any way!'

His mouth tilted in a cynical smile. 'I wonder what your fiancé would say if he saw how you just responded to me?'

Ashleigh felt as if someone had switched on a radiator behind her cheeks. Guilty colour burnt through her skin, making her feel transparent, as if he could see right through her to where she hid her innermost secrets.

She had to turn away, her back rigid with fury, as she glared at a painting on the wall in her line of vision.

'Oh, my God…' She stepped towards the portrait, her eyes growing wide with amazement, incredulity and what only could be described as gobsmacked stupefaction as realisation gradually dawned. Her eyes dipped to look at the signature at the bottom of the painting, even her very fingertips icing up with excitement as she turned around to look at him.

'Do you realise what you have here?' she asked, her tone breathless with wonder. 'That painting alone is worth thousands!'

He gave the painting a dismissive glance and met her eyes once more. 'You can have it,' he said. 'And everything else. There's more in the other rooms.'

She stared at him for at least five heavy heartbeats. *'What?'*

'You heard,' he said. 'I'm giving it to you to sell; everything in this house.'

She felt like slapping the side of her head to make sure she wasn't imagining what she'd just heard. 'What did you say?'

'I said I'm giving you the lot,' he said.

She backed away, her instincts warning her that this was not a no-strings deal. 'Oh, no.' She held up her hands as if to warn him off. 'You can't bribe me with a whole bunch of priceless heirlooms.'

'I'm not bribing you, Ashleigh,' he said in an even tone. 'I'm simply giving you a choice.'

'A choice?' She eyeballed him suspiciously. 'What sort of choice?'

His eyes gave nothing away as they held her gaze.

'I told you I wanted to see you again,' he said. 'Regularly.'

Ashleigh's heart began to gallop behind the wall of her chest. 'And I told you I can't…' She took a prickly breath.

'Howard and I…' She couldn't finish the sentence, the words sticking together in her tightened throat.

He gave her a cynical little smile that darkened his eyes even further. 'I don't think Howard Caule will protest at you spending time with me sorting this house out. In fact, I think he will send you off each day with his blessing.'

Cold fear leaked into her bloodstream and it took several precious seconds to locate her voice. 'W-what are you talking about?'

'I want you to spend the next month with me, sorting out my father's possessions.'

'I can't do that!' she squeaked in protest.

'Fine, then.' He reached for his mobile phone and began punching in some numbers. 'I'll call up another antiques dealer I know who will be more than happy to take this lot off me.' His finger was poised over the last digit as he added, 'For free.'

Ashleigh swallowed as he raised the phone to his ear.

He was giving the lot away? *For nothing?*

She couldn't allow him to do that. It wouldn't be right. The place was stacked to the rafters with priceless heirlooms. She owed Howard this deal for all he had done for her and Lachlan. She couldn't back out of it, no matter what it cost her personally.

'No!' She pulled his arm down so he couldn't continue the call. 'Wait… Let me think about this…'

He pocketed the phone. 'I'll give you thirty minutes to think it over. I should at this point make it quite clear that I'm not expecting you to sleep with me.'

She blinked at him, her tingling fingers falling away from his arm as his words sank in.

He didn't want her.

She knew she should be feeling relief but instead she felt

regret. An aching, burning regret that what they'd had before was now gone…

He continued in an even tone. 'We parted on such bitter terms four and a half years ago. This is a way for both of us to get some much needed closure.'

'But…but I don't need closure,' she insisted. 'I'm well and truly over you.'

He held her defiant look with enviable ease while her pulse leapt beneath her skin as she stood uncertainly before him.

'But I do,' he said.

Her mouth opened and closed but no sound came out.

Jake stepped back towards the door, holding it open as he addressed her in a coolly detached tone. 'I will leave you to make your initial assessment in private. When the thirty minutes are up I'll be back for your decision.'

Ashleigh stared at the back of the door once he'd closed it behind him, the echo of its lock clicking into place ringing in her ears for endless minutes.

A month!

A month in Jake's presence, sorting through the house he'd spent his childhood in.

She turned back around and stared at the fortune of goods in front of her, each and every one of them seeming to conceal a tale about Jake's past, their secrets locked within the walls of this old neglected house.

Why was he as good as throwing it all away? What possible reason could he have for doing so? Surely he would want to keep something back for himself? She knew he was a rich man now, but surely even very wealthy people didn't walk away from a veritable fortune?

Ashleigh sighed and turned, her eyes meeting those of the subject in the portrait on the wall. She felt a little feather of unease brush over her skin, for it seemed that every time she tried to move out of range of the oil-painted sad eyes they continued to follow her.

She gave herself a mental shake and rummaged in her bag for her digital camera. The sooner she got started the sooner she would be finished.

Her stomach gave a little flutter of nerves. There was something about this house that unsettled her and the less time she spent in it the better.

Especially with Jake here with her…

Alone…

CHAPTER THREE

ONCE she'd taken some preliminary photos Ashleigh left the overcrowded room for some much needed air and found herself wandering down the long passage, her thoughts flying off in all directions.

This was Jake's childhood home, the place where he had been raised, but for some reason it didn't seem to her to be the sort of house where a child would be particularly welcome.

This house seemed to be almost seeping with the wounds of neglect; the walls spoke of it with their faded peeling paint, the floorboards with their protesting creaks, as if her very tread had caused them discomfort as she moved across their tired surface. She could sense it in the woodwork of the furniture, the heavy layer of dust lying over every surface speaking of long-term disregard. And she could feel it in the reflection of the dust-speckled glass at the windows, the crumpled drape of the worn curtains looking as if they were doing their best to shield the house's secrets from the rest of the quiet conservative street.

Ashleigh had never considered herself a particularly intuitive person. That had been Ellie's role in the Forrester family, but somehow, being in Jake's childhood home made her realise things about him that had escaped her notice before.

He hated the darkness.

Why hadn't she ever noticed the significance of that before?

He had always been the first one to turn on the lights when they got home, insisting the blinds be pulled up even when the sunlight was too strong and disrupted the television or computer screen.

He'd hated loud music with a passion, particularly classical music. She couldn't remember a time when he hadn't come in and snapped her music off, glaring at her furiously, telling her it was too loud for the neighbours and why wasn't she being more responsible?

What did it all mean?

She opened another door off the hall and stepped inside. Some pinpricks of light were shining through the worn blinds, giving the room an eerie atmosphere, the dust motes disturbed by the movement of air as the door opened rising in front of her face like a myriad miniature apparitions.

The air was stuffy and close but she could see as she turned on the nearest light that it was some sort of study-cum-library, two banks of bookshelves lining the walls from floor to ceiling.

She moved across the old carpet to examine some of the titles, her eyes widening at the age of some of them nearest her line of vision.

Jake's father had sure known how to collect valuable items, she mused as she reached for what looked like a first edition of Keats's poems.

She put the book back amongst the others and turned to look around the rest of the room. The solid cedar desk was littered with papers as if someone working there had been interrupted and hadn't returned to put things in order. She picked up the document nearest her and found it was a financial statement from a firm of investors, the value of the portfolio making her head spin.

She heard a sound behind her and turned to see Jake standing in the frame of the door, his dark gaze trained on her.

Her time was up.

She put the paper back down on the desk, her mouth suddenly dry and uncooperative when there was so much she wanted to ask him before she committed herself to the task he had assigned her.

'Jake…I…I don't know what to say.' She waved a weak hand to encompass the contents of the room, the house and the sense of unease she'd felt as she'd moved through each part but not really knowing why.

'What's to say?' he said, moving into the room. 'My father died a very rich man.'

She gave a small frown as she recalled their conversation at his hotel the day before. 'I thought you intimated he left you nothing in his will?'

His eyes held hers for a brief moment before moving away. He wandered over to the big desk and, pulling out the throne-like chair, sat down, one ankle across his thigh, his hands going behind his head as he leaned backwards.

'He left me nothing I particularly wanted,' he answered.

Her teeth caught her bottom lip for a moment, her eyes falling away from the mysterious depths of his.

'But…we're not talking about a few old kitchen utensils and second-hand books here, Jake. This place is worth a fortune. The house itself on current market value would be enough to set anyone up for life, let alone the contents I've seen so far.'

'I'm not getting rid of the house, just what's inside it,' he informed her.

'You plan to live here?' She stared at him in surprise.

He unfolded his leg and stood up, his sudden increase in height making her feel small and vulnerable in the over-crowded space of the room.

'I have set up a branch of my company here in Sydney. I plan to spend half the year in England and the other half here.'

She moistened her mouth. 'But you told me earlier you've always hated this house.'

'I do.' He gave her another inscrutable look. 'But that's not to say it can't have a serious makeover and be the sort of home it should have been in the first place. I'm looking forward to doing it, actually.'

Ashleigh knew there was a wealth of information behind his words but she wasn't sure she was up to the task of asking him exactly what he meant. After all, hadn't he been the one who'd insisted on living in a low maintenance one-bedroom apartment when they had lived in London? Whatever was he going to do with a house this size, which looked as if it had at least ten bedrooms, several formal rooms, including a ball-room, not to mention an extensive front and back garden with a tennis court thrown in for good measure?

'It seems a bit…a bit big for a man who…' She let her words trail away when he moved towards her.

'For a man who what, Ashleigh?' he asked, picking up a strand of her shoulder-length hair and coiling it gently around his finger.

She swallowed as her scalp tingled at the gentle intimate tether of his finger in her hair, her heart missing a beat as his darker-than-night eyes secured hers.

'You're…you're a c-confirmed bachelor,' she reminded him, her tone far more breathy than she'd intended. 'No wife, no kids, no encumbrances, remember?'

His mouth lifted at one corner. 'You don't think it's pos-sible for people to change a little over time?'

Her heart gave another hard thump as she considered the most likely possibilities for his change of heart.

Perhaps he'd met someone…someone who was so perfect

for him he couldn't bear to live without her and was prepared to have her on any terms, even marriage—the formal state he had avoided so determinedly in the past.

She couldn't get the question past the blockage in her throat, but her mind tortured her by conjuring up an image of him standing at an altar with a beautiful bride stepping slowly towards him, his eyes alight with desire as the faceless woman drifted closer and closer to finally take his outstretched hand…

Jake uncoiled her hair but didn't move away.

Ashleigh tried to step backwards but her back and shoulders came up against the solid frame of the bookshelves. The old books shuffled on their shelves behind her and, imagining them about to tumble down all over her, she carefully edged away a fraction, but it brought her too close to Jake.

Way too close.

'W-what's…what's changed your mind?' she asked, surprised her voice came out sounding almost normal considering she couldn't inflate her lungs properly.

He stepped away from her and, picking up an old gold pen off the desk, began to twirl it in his fingers, his face averted from hers. It seemed to Ashleigh a very long time before he spoke.

'I have spent some time since my father's death thinking about my life. I want to make some changes now, changes I just wasn't ready to face before.' He put the pen down and faced her, his mouth twisted in a little rueful smile. 'It might sound strange to you, but you're the first person I've trusted enough to tell this to.'

Ashleigh felt her guilt claw at her insides with accusing fingers, sure if he looked too closely he would see the evidence of her betrayal splashed over her features.

She had kept from him the birth of his son.

What sort of trustworthiness had that demonstrated?

Jake turned away again as he continued heavily, 'But four

and a half years ago I just wasn't ready.' He raked a hand through his hair. 'I guess I'm only doing it now because my father is dead and buried.' He gave a humourless grunt of laughter and looked back at her. 'It's that closure I spoke of earlier.'

'So…' she ran her tongue over her desert-dry mouth '…have you changed your mind about…marriage?'

'I have given it some considerable thought,' he admitted, his eyes giving nothing away.

'What about the…the other things you were always so adamant about?' At his enquiring look she added, 'Kids, pets, that sort of thing.'

She picked up the faint sound of his breath being released as he turned to look out of the window over the huge back garden, the solid wall of his tall muscled frame instantly reminding her of an impenetrable fortress.

'No,' he said, reverting to the same flat emotionless tone he'd used earlier. 'I haven't changed my mind about that. I don't want children. Ever.'

Ashleigh felt the full force of his words as if he had punched them right through the tender flesh of her belly where his child had been curled for nine months. She hadn't realised how much she had hoped for a different answer until he'd given the one she'd most dreaded.

He didn't want children.

He *never* wanted children.

How could she tell him about his little son now?

Jake turned round to look at her. 'Have you decided to take me up on my offer, Ashleigh?' he asked.

'I—I need more time…'

'Sorry.' The hard glance he sent her held no trace of apology. 'Take it or leave it. If you want to have this stuff then you'll have to fulfil my terms. A month working nine to five in this house—alongside me.'

Panic set up an entire percussion section in Ashleigh's chest, the sickening thuds making her feel faint and the palms of her hands sticky with sweat.

'I—I don't usually work nine to five,' she said, avoiding his eyes.

'Oh, really?' There was a hint of surprise in his tone. 'Why ever not?'

'Howard doesn't like the thought of me working full-time,' she said, pleased with her response as it was as close to the truth as she could get.

'And you agreed to that?'

'I…' She lifted her chin a fraction. 'Yes. It frees me to do… other things.'

'What other things do you like doing?'

Ashleigh knew she had backed herself into a tight corner and the only way out of it was to lie. She averted her gaze once more and inspected a figurine near her with avid intent. 'I go to the gym.'

'The gym?' His tone was nothing short of incredulous.

Her chin went a bit higher as she met his eyes again. 'What are you saying, Jake? That I look unfit as well as fat?'

He held up his hands in a gesture of surrender. 'Hey, did I ever say you were fat?'

She threw him a resentful look and folded her arms across her chest. 'Yesterday when we met you said I'd put on weight. In my book that means you think I'm fat.'

She heard him mutter an expletive under his breath.

'I think you look fabulous.' His dark gaze swept over her, stalling a little too long for her comfort on the up-thrust of her breasts. 'You were a girl before, barely out of your teens. Now you're a woman. A sexy gorgeous-looking woman.'

Who has given birth to your son, Ashleigh wanted to add, but knew she couldn't.

Would she ever be able to?

'Thank you,' she mumbled grudgingly and looked away.

Jake gave an inward sigh.

He'd almost forgotten how sensitive she was. Her feelings had always seemed to him to be lying on the surface of her skin, not buried deep inside and out of reach as his mostly were.

But the Ashleigh he'd known in the past was certainly no gym junkie. Her idea of exercise had never been more than a leisurely walk, stopping every chance she could to smell any flowers that were hanging over the fence. It had driven him nuts at times. He needed the challenge of hard muscle-biting endurance exercise to keep his mind off the pain of things he didn't want to think about.

He still needed it.

'I'm prepared to negotiate on the hours you work,' he inserted into the silence.

Her head came up and he saw the relief in her blue eyes as they met his. 'Is…is ten to four all right?' she asked.

He pretended to think about it for a moment.

She shifted uncomfortably under his scrutiny and he wondered why she felt so ill at ease in his company. He'd expected a bit of residual anger, maybe even a good portion of bitterness, but not this outright nervousness. She was like a rabbit cornered in a yard full of ready-to-race greyhounds, her eyes skittering away from his, her small hands fluttering from time to time as if she didn't quite know what to do with them.

'Ten to four will be fine,' he said. 'Do you want me to pick you up each day?'

'*No!*'

One of his brows went upwards at her vehement response.

Ashleigh lowered her eyes and looked down at the twisting knot of her hands. 'I—I mean that won't be necessary. Besides—' she gave him a little speaking glance '—Howard wouldn't like that.'

'And what Howard wouldn't like good little Ashleigh wouldn't dream of doing, right?' he asked without bothering to disguise the full measure of scorn in his tone.

She clamped her lips shut, refusing to dignify his question with an answer.

'For Christ's sake, Ashleigh,' he said roughly. 'Can't you see he's all wrong for you?'

'Wrong?' She glared at him in sudden anger. 'How can you say that? It was you who was so wrong for me!'

'I wasn't wrong for you; I just—'

'You *were* wrong for me!' She threw the words at him heatedly. 'You ruined my life! You crushed my confidence and berated everything I held as important. I was your stupid plaything, something to pass the time with.'

'That's not true.' His voice was stripped of all emotion.

Ashleigh shut her eyes for a moment to hold back the threatening tears. She drew in a ragged breath and, opening her eyes again, sent him a glittering look. 'God damn you, Jake. How can you stand there and say Howard is all wrong for me when at least I can be myself with him? I could never be myself with you. You would never allow it.'

Jake found it hard to hold her accusing glare, his gut clenching at the vitriol in her words. As much as he hated admitting it, she was very probably right. He wasn't proud of how he had treated her in the past. He'd been insensitive and too overly protective of his own interests to take the time to truly consider hers.

The truth was she had threatened him from the word go.

He had always avoided the virginal, looking for hearth-home-and-cute hound-thrown-in types. He'd shied away from any form of commitment in relationships; the very fact that he'd let his guard down enough to allow her to move in with him demonstrated how much she had burrowed beneath his skin.

Her innocence had shocked him.

He had taken her roughly, their combined passion so strong and out of control he hadn't given a single thought to the possibility that it might have been her first time.

He'd hurt her and yet she hadn't cried. Instead she'd hugged him close and promised it would be better next time.

And it had been.

In fact, making love with Ashleigh had been an experience he was never likely to forget. She had given so freely of herself, the passion he'd awakened in her continually taking him by surprise. No one he'd been with since—and there had been many—had ever touched him quite the way she had touched him. Ashleigh had reached in with those small soft hands of hers to deep inside him where no one had ever been before. Sometimes, if he allowed himself, he could still feel where her gentle stroking fingertips had brushed along the torn edges of his soul.

'Ashleigh…' His voice sounded unfamiliar even to his own ears. He cleared his throat and continued. 'Can we just forget about the past and only deal with the here and now?'

Ashleigh brushed at her eyes with an angry gesture of her hand, hoping he wouldn't see how undone she really was. How could she possibly pretend the past hadn't happened when she had Lachlan to show for it?

'Why are you doing this?' she asked. 'What can you possibly hope to achieve by insisting I do this assessment for you? You say you don't want the money all this stuff is worth…' She drew in a scalding breath as her eyes scanned the goods in front of her before turning back to meet his steady gaze, her voice coming out a little unevenly. 'What exactly do you want?'

'This house is full of ghosts,' he said. 'I want you to help me get rid of them.'

She moistened her bone-dry lips. 'Why me?'

'I have my reasons,' he answered, his eyes telling her none of them.

Her gaze wavered on his for a long moment. This was all wrong. She couldn't help Jake deal with whatever issues he carried from his past. How could she when she had the most devastating secret of all, that at some point he would have to hear?

But he needs you, another voice inside her head insisted.

How could she turn away from the one man she had loved with all of her being? Surely she owed him this short period of time so he could achieve the closure he had spoken of earlier.

It was a risk she had to take. Spending any amount of time with Jake was courting trouble but as long as she stood her ground she would be fine.

She *had* to be fine.

'I think we need some ground rules then,' she said, attempting to be firm but falling well short of the mark.

'Rules?'

'Rules, Jake.' She sent him a reproachful look. 'Those moral parameters that all decent people live by.'

'All right, run them by me,' he said, the edge of his mouth lifted in a derisory smile.

She forced her shoulders back and met his gaze determinedly. 'There's to be no touching, for a start.'

'Fine by me.' He thrust his hands in his jeans pockets as if to remove the temptation right there and then.

Ashleigh had to drag her eyes away from the stretch of denim over his hands. 'And that includes kissing, of course,' she added somewhat primly.

He moistened his lips with his tongue as if removing the taste of her from his mouth. 'Of course.'

She straightened her spine, fighting to remain cool under that dark gaze as it ran over her. 'And none of those looks.'

'Which looks?' he asked, looking.

She set her mouth. '*That* look.'

'This look?' He pointed to his face, his expression all innocence.

She crossed her arms. 'You know exactly what I mean, Jake Marriott. You keep undressing me with your eyes.'

'I do?'

He did innocence far too well, she thought, but she could see the hunger reflected in his gaze and no way was she going to fuel it.

'You know you do and it has to stop. *Now.*'

He sent her one of his megawatt lazy smiles. 'If you say so.'

'I say so.'

He shifted his tongue inside his cheek for a moment. 'Are you done with your little rules?'

She gave him a schoolmarm look from down the delicate length of her nose. 'Yes. I think that just about covers it.'

'You want to hear my rules now?' he asked after a tiny heart-tripping pause.

Ashleigh gave a covert swallow and met his eyes with as much equanimity as she could muster. 'All right. If you must.'

'Good.'

Another little silence coiled around them.

Ashleigh didn't know where to look. For some strange reason, she wanted to do exactly what she'd just forbidden him to do.

She wanted to feast her eyes on his form.

She wanted to run her gaze over all the hot spots of his body, the hot spots she had set alight with her hands and mouth in the past.

She could almost hear the sound of his grunting pleasure in the silence throbbing between them, could almost feel the weight of him on her smaller frame as he pinned her beneath him.

She could almost feel the pulse of his spilling body between her legs, the essence of himself he had released at the moment of ecstasy, the full force of his desire tugging at her flesh both inside and out.

She forced herself to meet his coal-black gaze, her stomach instantly unravelling as she felt the heat coming off him towards her in searing scorching waves.

'I promise not to touch, kiss or even look if you promise to refrain from doing the same,' he stated.

I can do that, she thought. *I can be strong.*

I *have* to be strong.

'Not a problem,' she answered evenly. 'I have no interest in complicating things by revisiting our past relationship.'

'Fine. We'll start Monday at ten.' He took his hands out of his pockets and reached for a set of keys in the drawer of the desk and held them out to her like a lure.

'These are the keys to the house in case you get here before me,' he said.

She slowly reached out her opened palm and he dropped them into it.

'See? No touching.' He grinned down at her disarmingly.

She put the keys in her bag and straightened the strap on her shoulder to avoid his wry look. 'So far,' she muttered and turned towards the door.

'Ashleigh?'

She took an unsteady breath and turned back to face him. 'Yes?'

He held out the blood-red rose he'd picked for her earlier, the soft petals deprived of water for so long, already starting to wilt in thirst.

'You forgot this,' he said.

She found herself taking the four steps back to him to get her faded bloom, her fingers so meticulously avoiding his that she encountered a sharp thorn on the stem of the rose instead.

'Ouch!' She looked at the bright blood on her fingertip and began rummaging in her bag for a tissue, but before she could locate one Jake's hand came over hers and brought it slowly but inexorably up to his mouth.

She sucked in a tight little breath as he supped at the tiny pool of blood on her fingertip, her legs weakening as his eyes meshed with hers.

'Y-you promised…no t-touching…' she reminded him breathlessly but, for some inexplicable reason, didn't pull her finger out of his mouth.

She felt the slight rasp of his salving tongue, felt too the full thrust of her desire as it burst between her legs in hot liquid longing.

'I know.' He released her hand and stepped back from her. 'But you'll forgive me this once, won't you?'

She didn't answer.

Instead she turned on her heel and flew out the door and out of the house as if all the ghosts contained within were after her blood.

And not just one tiny little pin drop of it…

CHAPTER FOUR

LACHLAN flew out of the crèche playroom to greet her. 'Mummy! Guess what I did today?'

Ashleigh pressed a soft kiss to the top of his dark head and held him close for longer than normal, breathing in his small child smell. 'What did you do, my precious?'

He tugged on her hand and pulled her towards the painting room. 'I drewed a picture,' he announced proudly.

Ashleigh smiled and for once didn't correct his infant grammar. He would be four in a couple of months—plenty of time ahead to teach him. For now she wanted to treasure each and every moment of his toddlerhood.

It would all too soon be over.

'See?' He pressed a paint-splattered rectangle of paper into her hands.

She looked down at the stick-like figures he'd painted. 'Who's this?' she asked, bending down so she was on a level with him.

His chocolate-brown eyes met hers. 'That's Granny and Grandad.'

'And this one?' She pointed to another figure, who appeared to be doing some sort of dance.

'That's Auntie Mia,' he said.

I should have guessed that, Ashleigh thought wryly. Mia

was the Forrester fitness fanatic and was never still for a moment.

'And this one?' She knew who it was without asking. The dog-like drawing beside the blonde-haired human figure was a dead give-away but she wanted to extend his pleasure in showing off his work.

'That's Auntie Ellie.' He pointed to the yellow hair he'd painted. 'And that's one of the dogs she's wescued.'

Ashleigh's eyes centred on the last remaining figure who was standing behind all the others.

'Who is that?' she asked, not sure she really wanted to know.

'That's you,' he said, a touch of sadness creeping into his tone.

She swallowed the lump in the back of her throat and stared down at the picture. 'Really?'

'Yes.' He met her eyes with a look so like his father's she felt like crying.

'Why am I way back there?' She pointed to the background of his painting.

His eyes shifted away from hers, his small shoulders slumping as a small sigh escaped from his lips. 'I miss you, Mummy.'

'Oh, baby.' She clutched him to her chest, burying her head into the baby-shampoo softness of his hair, her eyes squeezing shut to hold the tears back. 'Mummy has to work, you know that, darling.' She eased him away from her and looked down into his up-tilted face. 'Aren't you happy at crèche and at the times you have with Granny and Grandad?'

His little chin wobbled for a moment before he got it under control. 'Yes…'

Ashleigh's stomach folded as she saw the insecurity played out on his features. Hadn't she seen that same look on Jake's face in the past, even though, like Lachlan, he had done his level best to hide it?

'I have to work, poppet,' she said. 'I have to provide for us. I can't expect Granny and Grandad to help us for ever.'

'But what about my daddy?' Lachlan asked. 'Doesn't he want to provide for me too?'

I will kill you, Mia, so help me God, she said under her breath. This was surely her sister's doing, for Lachlan had never mentioned anything about his father in the past.

'He doesn't know about you,' she said, deciding the truth was safer in the long run.

'Why not?'

She couldn't meet his eyes.

Was this how it was going to be for the rest of her life, guilt keeping her from looking at eyes that were the mirror image of his father's?

'I couldn't tell him…' she said at last.

'Why not, Mummy?'

She closed her eyes and counted to five before opening them again. 'Because he never wanted to be a daddy.'

'But I *want* a daddy,' he said, his big dark eyes tugging at Ashleigh's heartstrings. 'Do you think if I met him and asked him he would change his mind?'

She looked down at the tiny up-tilted face and smiled in spite of her pain. 'I just know he would. But you can't meet him, sweetie.'

'Why?'

She hugged him close, not sure how to answer.

'Mummy?'

'Mmm?' She bit the inside of her cheek to stop herself from falling apart.

'I still love my daddy even if he doesn't want to see me,' he said solemnly.

Ashleigh felt as if someone had just stomped on her heart.

* * *

Howard couldn't contain his delight at her decision to take on the assessment.

'You mean he wants to give us the whole lot?' he asked incredulously. *'For nothing?'*

She nodded, her expression unmistakably grim. 'That's the deal.'

'But on market value the whole load is probably worth...' He did a quick mental calculation from the notes Ashleigh had already prepared. 'Close to a couple of million, at the very least!'

'I know...' Her stomach tightened another notch. 'But he doesn't want any of it.'

'He's mad,' Howard said. 'Totally out of his mind, stark staring mad.'

Ashleigh didn't answer. She didn't think Jake was mad, just being incredibly tactical.

Howard frowned for a moment. 'Does he...' he cleared his throat as if even harbouring the thought offended him '...does he want something in exchange, apart from you working in the house to document everything?'

'What do you mean?' Ashleigh hoped her cheeks weren't as hot on the outside as they felt to her on the inside.

'Some men can be quite...er...ruthless at times, Ashleigh, in getting what they want,' he said. 'No one but no one gives away a fortune of goods without wanting something in return.'

'He doesn't want to sleep with me, if that's what's worrying you,' she said, wondering why it had hurt to say it out loud.

'He told you that?' Howard's red brows rose.

She nodded.

He let out a sigh of relief. 'You are doing me the biggest favour imaginable, Ashleigh.' He took her hands and squeezed them in his. 'This will secure our future. We can get married in grand style and never have to worry about making ends meet again. Think of it!' His face glowed with delight at this stroke of good fortune. 'My mother is thrilled. She wants you to come to dinner this evening to celebrate with us.'

Ashleigh felt like rolling her eyes. The one sticking point in her relationship with Howard, apart from his deeply ingrained conservatism, was his mother. No matter how hard she tried, she just did not like Marguerite Caule.

'I need to spend time with Lachlan,' she said carefully, removing her hands from his hold. 'He's been missing me lately.'

'Bring him with you,' Howard suggested. 'You know how much my mother enjoys seeing him.'

Seeing him, but not hearing him, Ashleigh added under her breath. Marguerite was definitely from the old school of child-rearing: children were to be seen not heard, and if it could possibly be avoided without direct insult, not interacted with at all.

'Maybe some other time,' she said, avoiding his pleading look. 'I have a lot on my mind just now.'

She heard him sigh.

'Is this all too much for you?' he asked. 'Do you want me to call Jake Marriott and pull out on the deal? I know it's a lot of money but if you aren't up to it then I won't force you.'

Ashleigh turned to look at him, privately moved by his concern. He was such a lovely person, no hint of malice about him. He loved Lachlan and he loved her.

Why, oh, why, couldn't she love him in return?

He had so much to lose on this. His business hung in the balance. It was up to her to save it. She couldn't walk away from Jake's deal without hurting Howard, and hurting him was the last thing she wanted to do.

Besides, it *was* a lot of money to throw away. How could

she live with herself if she turned her back on Jake's offer, no matter what motive had precipitated it?

'No…' She picked up her bag and keys resignedly. 'I'm going to see this through. I think Jake is right.' She gave a rough-edged sigh. 'I need closure.'

'Good luck.'

She gave him a rueful look as she reached for the door. 'Luck has been in short supply in my life. I hardly see it changing any time soon.'

'Don't worry, Ashleigh,' Howard reassured her. 'He's given you the opportunity of a lifetime. Don't let your past relationship with him get in the way of your future with me.'

Ashleigh found it hard to think of an answer. Instead she sent him a vague smile and left the showroom, somehow sensing that her future was always going to be inextricably linked with Jake.

Even if by some miracle he never found out about Lachlan.

The house and grounds were deserted when Ashleigh arrived. Jake's car was nowhere in sight and, although most of the blinds at the windows hadn't been pulled completely down, the house still gave off a deserted, abandoned look.

She walked up the cracked pathway to the front door, feeling as if she was stepping over an invisible barrier into the privacy of Jake's past.

She rang the doorbell just in case, but there was no answer. She listened as the bell echoed down the hall like an aching cry of loneliness, the sound bouncing off the walls and coming back to her as if to taunt her. She put the key into the lock and turned it, the door opening under her hand with a groan of protest.

At least it didn't smell as musty as before.

The movement of air in the hall indicated that Jake had left a window open and she couldn't help a soft sigh of remembrance. Hadn't he always insisted on sleeping with at least one window open, even when it had been freezing cold outside?

She wandered from room to room, taking a host of pictures with a digital camera, stopping occasionally to carefully document notes on the various pieces, her fingers flying over the notebook in her hand as she detailed the estimated date and value of each item.

As treasure troves went, this was one of the biggest she'd ever encountered. Priceless piece after priceless piece was noted on her list, her estimation growing by the minute. Howard's business would be lifted out of trouble once these babies hit the showroom floor.

She lifted the hair out of the back of her top and rolled her stiff shoulders as she finished the first room. She glanced at her watch and saw it was now well after twelve. Two hours had gone past and still no sign of Jake.

Deciding to take a break, she left her notebook and pen on a side table and wandered through to the kitchen at the back of the house.

It wasn't the sort of kitchen in which she felt comfortable. It was dark and old-fashioned, the appliances so out of date she wondered if they were still operational.

She picked up a lonesome cup that someone, she presumed Jake's father, had left on the kitchen sink. It was heavily stained with the tannin of tea, the chipped edge seeming out of place in a house so full of wealth. She ran her fingertip over the rough edge thoughtfully, wondering what sort of man Jake's father had been.

Ashleigh realised with a little jolt that she had never seen a picture of either of his parents, had never even been informed of their Christian names.

She thought of the stack of family albums her mother had lovingly put together. Every detail of family life was framed with openly adoring comments. There were shiny locks of hair and even tiny pearly baby teeth.

What had Jake's parents looked like? She hadn't a clue and yet their blood was surging through her son's veins.

'I'm sorry I'm so late,' Jake said from just behind her.

Ashleigh swung around, surprise beating its startled wings inside her chest. 'I wish you would stop doing that,' she said, clutching at her leaping throat.

'Do what?' He looked at her blankly.

She lowered her hand and gave herself a mental shake. 'You should announce your arrival a bit more audibly. I hate being sneaked up on like that.'

'I did not sneak up on you,' he said. 'I called out to you three times but you didn't answer.'

She bit her lip, wondering if what he said was true. It was certainly possible given that her thoughts had been located well in the past, but it still made her feel uncomfortable that he could slip through her firewall of defences undetected.

She put the cup she'd been holding down and turned away from his probing gaze. 'I've almost finished assessing one room.'

'And?'

Her eyes reluctantly came back to his. 'Your father certainly knew what he was doing when it came to collecting antiques.'

He gave a humourless smile. 'My father was an expert at many things.'

Again she sensed the wealth of information behind the coolly delivered statement.

'Would it help to…to talk about it?' she asked, somewhat tentatively.

His eyes hardened beneath his frowning brow. 'About what?'

'About your childhood.'

He swung away from her as if she'd slapped him. 'No, not right now.'

She bit her lip, not sure if she should push him. A part of her wanted to. She ached to know what had made him the man he was, but another part of her warned her to let well alone. His barriers were up again. She could see it in the tense line of his jaw and the way his eyes moved away from hers as if he was determined to shut her out.

'Which room would you like me to work on next?' She opted for a complete change of subject.

He gave a dismissive shrug and shoved at a dirty plate on the work table in front of him as if it had personally offended him.

'I don't care. You choose.'

'Which room was your bedroom?' she asked before she could stop herself.

She saw the way his shoulders stiffened, the rigidity of his stance warning her she had come just a little too close for comfort.

'I don't want you to go in there,' he said. 'The door is locked and it will stay that way. Understood?'

She forced herself to hold his glittering glare. 'If that's what you want.'.

He gave her one diamond-hard look and moved past her to leave the room. 'I will be in the back garden. I have some digging to do.'

She sighed as the door snapped shut behind him.

What had she taken on?

It was well after three p.m. when she decided she needed a break. She had nibbled on a few crackers she'd brought with her and had a glass of water earlier, but her eyes were watering from all the dust she'd disturbed as she itemised the contents of the largest formal room.

She went out the back door, her eyes automatically searching the garden for Jake as she sat down on one of the steps, stretching her legs out to catch the sun.

He was down in the far corner, his back and chest bare as he dug up the ground beneath the shade of the elm tree. She saw the way his toned muscles bunched with each strike of the spade in the resisting earth, the fine layer of perspiration making his skin gleam in the warm spring sunshine.

He stopped and, leaning on the spade, wiped a hand across his sweaty brow, his eyes suddenly catching sight of her watching him.

He straightened and, stabbing the spade into the ground, walked towards her, wiping his hands on the sides of his jeans.

From her seated position on the back step she had to crane her neck to look up at him. 'That looks like hard work,' she said. 'Do you want me to get you a glass of water?'

He shook his head. 'I drank from the tap a while ago.'

She lowered her gaze, then wished she hadn't as she encountered the zipper of his jeans. She jerked upright off the step but her sandal caught in the old wire shoe-scraper and she pitched forwards.

Jake caught her easily, hauling her upright, his hands on her upper arms almost painfully firm.

'Are you OK?'

'I—I'm fine…' She tried to ease herself out of his hold but he countered it with a subtle tightening of his fingers.

She had no choice but to meet his eyes. 'You can let me go now, Jake.'

Tiny beads of perspiration were peppered over his upper lip, a dark smudge of soil slashed across the lean line of his jaw giving him an almost primitive look. Gone was the high-powered architect who had offices in several major cities of the world; in his place was a man who smelt of hard physical work and fitness, his chest so slick with sweat she wanted to press her mouth to his skin and taste his saltiness.

His hands dropped away from her and he stepped backwards. 'I've made you dirty,' he said without apology.

She glanced at each of her arms, her stomach doing a funny little tumble turn when she saw the full set of his earthy fingerprints on the creamy skin of her bare upper arms.

'It's all right,' she said. 'At least I wasn't wearing the jacket. I left it inside it was so…so hot…'

His eyes ran over her neat skirt and matching camisole and she wished she hadn't spoken. She could feel the weight of his gaze as it took in her shadowed cleavage, a cleavage she hadn't had four and a half years ago.

'I'd better get back to work…' she said, waving a hand at the house behind her, her feet searching blindly for the steps. 'There's still so…so much to do and I need to leave on time.'

'If you want to leave early, that's fine,' he said, narrowing his eyes against the sun as he looked back over the garden. 'I'm just about finished for the day myself.'

Ashleigh hovered on the first step. 'What are you going to plant in that garden bed you're digging?'

It seemed an age before his gaze turned back to meet hers, his eyes so dark and intense she felt the breath trip somewhere in the middle of her throat.

'I'm not going to plant anything.'

A nervous hand fluttered up to her neck, her fingers holding the fine silver chain hanging there, her expression clouded with confusion. 'Then what are you digging for?'

His mouth tilted into one of his humourless smiles.

'Memories, Ashleigh,' he said, his tone deep and husky. 'I'm digging for memories.'

Ashleigh watched him, her eyes taking in the angles and planes of his face, wondering what was going on behind the screen of his inscrutable gaze.

He'd always been so adept at concealing his true feelings; it had both frustrated and fascinated her in the past. She knew his aloofness was part of what fed her lingering attraction for him. She felt ashamed of how she felt, especially given her commitment to Howard, but every time she was in Jake's presence she felt the pull of something indefinable, as if he had set up a special radar to keep her tuned in to him, only him. She felt the waves of connection each time his gaze meshed with hers, the full charge zapping her whenever he touched her. His kiss had burnt her so much she was sure if it were to be repeated she would never have the strength to pull away. It wouldn't matter how committed she was elsewhere, when Jake Marriott's mouth came down on hers everyone else ceased to exist.

'You're breaking rule number three,' Jake's voice cut through her private rumination. 'No looks, remember?'

She dragged her eyes away from the amused line of his mouth and met his eyes, her cheeks heating from the inside like a stoked furnace.

'I wasn't *looking*, I was thinking,' she insisted.

'One wonders what was going on in that pretty little head of yours to make you blush so delightfully,' he mused.

'I'm not blushing!' She flung her hair back with a defiant toss of one hand. 'It's hot. You know how I can't stand the heat. You always said I…' She stopped speaking before she trawled up too many dangerous memories. She didn't want him thinking she had stored away every single word he'd ever spoken to her.

'I always said what?'

'Nothing; I can't remember.' She carefully avoided his eyes. 'It was all such a long time ago.'

'Four years is not such a long time.'

'Four and a half,' she said, meeting his eyes with gritty determination. 'Time to move on, don't you think?'

'That's why we're here,' he said. 'So we can both move on.'

'Then let's get on with it,' she suggested and turned towards the house.

'Ashleigh.'

She sent her eyes heavenward with a silent prayer for strength as she turned to look back at him. Because she was on the top step he was now at eye level. This close she could see the curling fringe of his sooty lashes, could even feel the movement of air against her lips when he let out a small breath. Her stomach muscles tightened, her legs going to water at his physical proximity. She had only to tilt her body a mere fraction and she would be touching him.

No touching, she reminded herself firmly.

Rule number one.

Her gaze dipped to the curve of his mouth and she mentally chanted rule number two, over and over again. *No kissing, no kissing, no kissing, no—*

'I want to visit your family,' Jake said, startling her out of her chant. 'I was thinking about coming over this evening.'

'*What?*' She choked. 'W-whatever for?'

He gave her a long studied look, taking in her flustered features and fluttering nervous hands.

Ashleigh fought her panic under some semblance of control as her mind whirled with a list of possible excuses for putting him off. She straightened her shoulders, controlled her hands by tying them together and forced herself to meet his eyes.

'We're all busy,' she said. 'No one's going to be home.'

'Tomorrow will do just as well.'

'That's no good either,' she said quickly—far too quickly.

He gave her a sceptical look. 'What happened to the happy-to-be-at-home-altogether-every-night Forrester family? I thought your family's idea of a big night out was once a month to the cinema.'

She set her mouth, knowing he was mocking the stable security of her family. 'My parents have regular evenings out and so do my sisters,' she said, not bothering to hide the defensiveness in her tone. 'Anyway, I will be out with Howard.'

'I don't need you to be there,' he said.

No, but if he were to see even a single toy of Lachlan's lying about the house he would begin to ask questions she wasn't prepared to answer. Not to mention all the photographs arranged on just about every surface and wall by her overly sentimental mother. She'd been lucky the first time when he'd called in unexpectedly but she could hardly strip the house of everything with Lachlan's name or face on it.

'All the same, I don't think it's such a good idea.' She bit her lip momentarily as she hunted her brain for a reasonable excuse. 'My parents are…very loyal and since we…I mean… you and I parted on such bitter terms they might not be all that open to seeing you now.'

'Your mother was fine with me the other day,' he said. 'Admittedly she didn't ask me in for tea and scones, but she was openly friendly and interested in how I was doing.'

I will throttle you, Mum, for being so damned nice all the time, she silently vowed.

'I don't think Howard would like the thought of you fraternising with my family,' she put in desperately.

The cynical smirk reappeared at the mention of her fiancé's name.

'We don't have to tell Howard,' he said, adding conspiratorially with the wink of one dark glittering eye, 'it can be our little secret.'

Ashleigh was already sick to death of secrets, her one and only one had caused enough anguish to last a lifetime. She felt as if her heart hadn't had a normal rhythm in days and even now her head was constantly pounding with the tension of trying to avoid a vocal slip in Jake's presence.

'I'd rather not do anything behind Howard's back,' she said.

'Good little Ashleigh,' he drawled with unmistakable mockery.

She ground her teeth and wished she could slap that insolent look off his face, but she knew if she did all three rules would end up being broken right there and then where they stood on the back door steps.

She straightened her spine, speaking through tight lips. 'I'll arrange a meeting for you with my family on neutral ground. A restaurant or something like that some time next week or the one after.'

He inclined his head at her in a gesture of old-world politeness. 'If you insist.'

'I do.'

'Why don't you and Howard join the party?' he suggested.

'I don't think so.'

He gave a soft chuckle of laughter. 'Why? Would he be frightened he might have to foot the bill?'

She sent him an arctic glare. 'Howard is a hard-working man. Sure, he doesn't have the sort of money that you do to throw around, but at least he is honest and up-front.'

'What are you implying? That I came by my fortune by less than honest means?' His eyes were hard as they lasered hers.

'How did you do it, Jake?' she asked. 'When we were living in London you hardly had a penny to your name.'

'I worked hard and had some lucky breaks,' he said. 'No shady deals, so you can take that look of disapproval off your face right now.'

'From living in squalor to billionaire in four and a half years?' she gave him a disbelieving look. 'You should write one of those how-to-be-successful books.'

'I didn't exactly live in squalor,' he said.

'No, not after I moved in and did all your housework for

you,' she bit out resentfully. 'How delightfully convenient for you, a housekeeper and lover all rolled into one.'

Ashleigh felt his continued silence as if it were crawling all the way up her spine to lift the fine hairs on the back of her neck.

She knew she was cornered. Her back was already up against the closed door behind her and his tall frame in front of her blocked any other chance of escape.

She could feel the air separating them pulsing with banked up emotions. Dangerous emotions, emotions that hadn't been unleashed in a very long time…

CHAPTER FIVE

ASHLEIGH could feel the weight of his dark gaze on her mouth, the sensitive skin of her lips lifting, swelling as if in search of the hard pressure of his, her heart fluttering behind her ribcage as his head came even closer.

'Don't even think about it…' she cautioned him, her voice a cracked whisper of sound as it passed through her tight throat.

His lips curved just above hers, hovering tantalisingly close, near enough to feel the brush of his warm breath as he asked, 'Is that to be another one of your little rules?'

She moistened her lips nervously. 'Yes…' She cleared her throat. 'Rule number four: don't think about me in that way.'

'How do you know what way I'm thinking about you?' His dark eyes gleamed with mystery.

'You're still a full-blooded man, aren't you?' she asked with considerable tartness. 'Or is that another one of those changes you insist you've undergone in the last four and a half years?'

He had timed silences down to a science, Ashleigh thought. He used them so tactically. She had forgotten just how tactically.

She held her breath, waiting for him to say something, her head getting lighter and lighter as each pulsing second passed.

'Want to check for yourself?' he finally asked.

'What?' Her indrawn breath half-inflated her lungs and her head swam alarmingly as his meaning gradually dawned on her.

He pointed to his groin, her eyes following the movement of his hand as if they had a mind of their own.

'You're the expert assessor. Why don't you head south to check out if the crown jewels are still in mint condition?'

Her eyes flew back to his in a flash of anger. 'This is all a big game to you, isn't it, Jake? You think this is so funny with your stupid double meanings and sexual hints.' She sucked in a much needed breath and continued, 'I'm not interested. Got that? Not in-ter-est-ed. Do I have to spell it out for you? Why can't you hear what I'm telling you?'

'There seems to be some interference from the transmission centre,' he said.

'Transmiss…' She rolled her eyes. 'Oh, for God's sake! Is your ego so gargantuan that you can't accept that what we had is over?'

'It would be a whole lot easier to accept if you didn't look at me with those hungry eyes of yours,' he said.

'Hungry eyes?' She gaped at him in affront. 'You're the one with the wandering eyes!'

'I said hungry, not wandering.'

'Don't split hairs with me!' she spat back. 'And back off a bit, will you?' She leant back even further against the door behind her until the door handle began to dig into the tender flesh of her lower back. 'I can practically see what you had for breakfast.'

'I didn't have breakfast.'

'Do you think I care?' she asked.

He gave her one of his lengthy contemplative looks. Ashleigh could feel herself dissolving under his scrutiny. She felt as if he could see through her skin to where her heart was beating erratically in response to his closeness.

'See?' He held up his hands as if he'd just read her mind. 'I'm not touching you.'

'You don't have to; just being close to you is enough to—' She clamped her wayward mouth shut and sent him another furious glare.

'Is enough to what, Ashleigh?' he asked, his deep voice like a length of sun-warmed silk being passed over too sensitive skin.

She refused to answer, tightening her mouth even further.

'Tempt you?' he prompted.

'I'm not the least bit tempted,' she said, wishing to God it was true.

'That's what the rules are for, aren't they, Ashleigh?' he taunted her softly. 'They're not for me at all. They're for you, to remind you of your commitment to dear old Howard.'

'He is not old!' she put in defensively. 'He's younger than you. He's thirty and you're thirty-three.'

'How very sweet of you to remember how old I am.'

Damn! She chided herself. She hadn't seen that coming and had fallen straight into it.

'If you don't mind I'd like to get on with what I'm supposed to be doing,' she said, hitching up her chin.

He stepped down a step and her breath whooshed out in relief. He didn't speak, but simply turned away to stride down to the back of the garden to the spade he'd dug into the earth under the elm, lifting it out of the ground and resuming his digging as if the last few minutes hadn't occurred.

Ashleigh tore her eyes away from the sculptured contours of his muscles and, wrenching open the back door, hurried inside where, for once, the dark lurking shadows of the house didn't seem quite so threatening.

Her father was the first person she saw when she got home that afternoon after picking up Lachlan from the crèche.

'I need to talk to you, Dad,' she said, hanging up Lachlan's backpack on the hook behind the kitchen door.

'Where's Lachlan?' Heath Forrester asked.

'He wanted to play outside for a while,' she informed him with undisguised relief. Her young son had been full of energy and endless chatter all the way home from the crèche and it had nearly driven her crazy.

Heath gave her a look of fatherly concern. 'What's on your mind, or should I say who?'

Her breath came out on the back of a deep sigh. 'Jake wants to have a family get-together of all things.'

Heath's bushy brow rose expressively. 'That could be a problem.'

She sent him a speaking glance as she reached for the kettle. 'He wanted to come here tonight but I managed to put him off. I said I'd organise a restaurant for some other evening in a week or two.' She leant her hips back against the bench as the kettle started heating. 'I just wish I didn't have to deal with this. I can't think straight when he's…when he's around.'

'You share a past with him,' her father said. 'It won't go away, especially with Lachlan lying between you.'

'You think I should tell him, don't you?'

Heath compressed his lips in thought for a moment. 'Jake's a difficult man, but not an unreasonable one, Ashleigh. For all you know he might turn out to be a great father if given the chance.'

'But he's always made it more than clear he never wanted to have children,' she said. 'He told me the very same thing again yesterday.'

'He might think differently if he met Lachlan,' Heath said.

Ashleigh smiled sadly in spite of her disquiet. 'You and Mum are the most devoted grandparents I know. Of course you would think that, but I know Jake. He would end up hating Lachlan for having the audacity to be born without his express permission.'

'I understand your concerns but you can't hide Lachlan from him for ever,' Heath pointed out. 'Attitudes have changed these days. He has a legal right to know he has fathered a child.'

'I know…' Ashleigh sighed. 'But I can't do it now. Not like this. I need more time. I need to prepare myself, not to mention Lachlan.'

'Who is going to prepare Jake?' Heath asked.

'That's not my responsibility,' she said.

Her father didn't answer but reached for two cups in silence. Ashleigh dropped two tea bags into the cups he put on the bench in front of her and poured the boiling water over them, watching as the clear liquid turned brown as the tea seeped from the bags into the water.

'I *will* tell him, Dad,' she addressed the cup nearest her, 'eventually.'

'I know you will,' her father answered, taking his cup. 'But I just hope it's not going to be too late.'

Ashleigh stared into the cup in her hands, the darkness of her tea reminding her of Jake's fathomless eyes—eyes that could cut one to the quick or melt the very soul.

'Better late than never…' she murmured.

'That's certainly a well-used adage,' Heath said. 'But I wonder what Jake will think?'

Ashleigh just gave her father a twisted grimace as she lifted her cup to her lips. She spent most of her sleepless nights tortured by imagining what Jake would think.

It wasn't a pretty picture.

'So how is your assessment going?' Howard asked her the next morning.

Ashleigh handed him the notes she'd made so far. 'I've

done one room, mostly the furniture as I think I'll need your help with the figurines. I've looked them up in the journals but I'd prefer your opinion. The painting, however, is certainly an Augustus Earle original. I think there are more but the one I've seen so far is worth a mint.'

'Good work,' Howard congratulated her as he glanced over her descriptions.

'I've taken some initial digital photos but I haven't downloaded them yet,' she said. 'It's a big house and the furniture is virtually stacked to the ceiling in some rooms. It will take me most of the next week to get everything photographed and documented.'

'So how is it working alongside your ex-boyfriend?'

Ashleigh found it hard to meet Howard's gently enquiring gaze. 'It's all right…I guess.'

'He hasn't—' he paused, as if searching for the right word '—made a move on you, has he?'

'Of course not!' she denied hotly.

Howard gave her a slightly shamefaced look. 'Sorry, just asking. You know I trust you implicitly.'

She stretched her mouth into a tight smile that physically hurt. 'Thank you.'

'However, I'm not sure I trust him,' he continued as if she hadn't spoken.

'You've only met him the once; surely that's not enough time to come to any sort of reasonable opinion on someone's character.' She found it strange springing to Jake's defence but it irked her to think her fiancé had made that sort of critical judgement without a fair trial.

'I know the type,' Howard answered. 'Too much money, too much power, not enough self-restraint.'

That about sums it up, she thought to herself, but decided against telling him how close he'd come to assessing her ex-lover's personality.

'I thought you were glad he was giving us this load of goods?' she said.

'I am,' he said. 'More than glad, to be honest. Who wouldn't be? It's a dream come true. Without this input of goods I was going to be sailing a little too close to the wind for my liking. The antiques fair coming up will time in nicely with this little haul. I will make a fortune out of it.'

'If it goes through,' she muttered darkly.

'What do you mean?' Howard looked at her in consternation.

'What if he pulls on the deal?'

'Why would he do that?' he asked. 'He gave us the exclusive. Well, at least he gave it to you.' He glanced at her narrowly. 'You're not making things difficult for him, are you?'

'Why would I do that?'

He gave a shrug. 'You're very bitter about him. Up until the other day you never once mentioned his name in the whole time I've known you.'

'You didn't ask.' She kept herself busy with shuffling some papers on her desk.

'That's because I sensed it was too painful for you,' he said.

Ashleigh looked at him, her expression softening as she recalled the way he had always considered her feelings. He was like the older brother she'd always wanted—caring, considerate and concerned for her at all times.

'I'm hoping he won't pull out of the deal.' She picked up a pen and rolled it beneath her fingers, the line of her mouth grim. 'But who knows what he might do if he finds out about Lachlan?' She stared at the pen for a moment before adding, 'He seems keen to get his father's house cleaned out so he can start renovating it.' She gave a tiny despondent sigh and added, 'I think I'm what you could call part of his clean-up process.'

'What do you mean?'

The pen rolled out of her reach. A small frown creased her brow as she lifted her gaze back to his. 'I can't quite work him out. Sometimes I think he wants to talk to me about his past…I mean *really* talk. You know, tell me every detail. But then he seems to close up and back off as if I've come too close.'

'It's a difficult time when a parent passes away,' Howard said. 'I remember when my father died how hard it was. I was torn between wanting to talk and needing to stay silent in case I couldn't handle the emotion.'

Ashleigh chewed her bottom lip for a moment. 'I could be wrong, but I can't help feeling he isn't exactly grieving his father's passing.'

'Oh?' Howard frowned. 'You mean they didn't get on or something?'

'I don't know…but why else would he be practically giving away everything his father left him?'

Howard let out a breath. 'I guess it wouldn't hurt to listen to him if he ever decides he wants to tell you about it. What harm could it do? You never know, you might come to see him in a totally new light.'

Ashleigh gave him a small wan smile by way of response. She didn't want to see Jake Marriott in a new light.

She didn't want to see Jake Marriott at all.

It wasn't safe.

'Come on!' Mia urged Ashleigh on the cross-training machine at the local gym early the next morning. 'Use those legs now, up and down, up and down.'

Ashleigh grimaced against the iron weight of her thighs and continued, sweat pouring off her reddened face and pooling between her breasts. 'I thought this was supposed to fun,' she gasped in between steps.

'It is once you get fit,' Mia said, springing on to the treadmill alongside.

Ashleigh watched in silent envy as her trim and toned sister deftly punched in the directions on the treadmill and began running at a speed she'd thought only greyhounds could manage.

'You make me sick,' she said with mock sourness as she clung to the moving handles of the machine, her palms slippery and her legs feeling like dead pieces of wood.

Mia gave her a sweet smile as she continued running. 'It's your fault for fibbing to Jake about going to the gym regularly.'

'Yeah, don't remind me.'

'Anyway, I think it's a great idea for you to get some exercise,' Mia said without even puffing. 'You're so busy juggling work and Lachlan that you don't get any time on your own. You know how much Mum and Dad love to mind him for you so there's no excuse. The gym is a great place to switch off.'

Ashleigh looked at the sea of sweaty bodies around her and seriously wondered if her sister was completely nuts. Loud music was thumping, a row of televisions were transmitting several versions of early morning news shows, and a muscle-bound personal trainer who looked as if he'd been fed steroids from birth was adding to the cacophony of noise by shouting out instructions to a middle-aged man with a paunch, in tones just like a drill sergeant at Boot Camp.

'I can't believe people get addicted to this,' she said with a pointed look at her sister.

Mia grinned. 'It's also a great place to meet people.' She glanced at a tall, exceptionally handsome man who was doing bench presses on the other side of the room. 'Not a bad sight for this time of the morning, is it?'

Ashleigh couldn't help thinking that Jake's muscles as he'd dug the garden the previous day were much more defined than the man in question; however, she had to accede that her sister was right. There were certainly worse things to be looking at first thing in the morning.

'How long do I have to do this for?' she asked after a few more excruciating minutes of physical torture.

'Five more minutes and then we'll do some stomach crunches,' Mia informed her cheerily.

Ashleigh slid a narrow-eyed glance her sister's way. 'How many?'

'Three hundred a day should do it,' Mia said determinedly. 'You're not overweight, just under-toned.'

'*Three hundred?*' Ashleigh groaned.

'Come on,' Mia said and, jumping off the treadmill, pulled over a floor mat near the mirrored wall. 'Down on the floor and let's get started.'

'One…two…three…four…five…'

When Ashleigh arrived at Jake's house later that morning the temperature had risen to the late thirties and the air was thick and cloying with humidity. A clutch of angry, bruised-looking clouds was already gathering on the western horizon as if in protest at the unseasonable heat.

She couldn't see Jake's car or any sign of him about the house or garden so she let herself in and closed the door with a sigh of relief as the coolness of the dark interior passed over her like a chilled breath of air.

She lost track of time as she went to work in the second of the two formal sitting rooms, this one smaller but no less jam-packed. She ran her hand over a Regency rosewood and brass-inlaid dwarf side cabinet in silent awe. The cabinet had a frieze drawer and a pleated cupboard door decorated with a brass grille and was on sabre supports. She knew it would fetch a fabulous price at auction and the very fact that Howard had it in his possession would lift his profile considerably.

Her gaze shifted to a George III mahogany cabinet, and then to a Victorian walnut credenza which was inlaid and gilt metal-mounted, the lugged serpentine top above a panelled cupboard door and flanked by glazed serpentine doors.

The scent of old wood stirred her nostrils as she took photo after photo, edging her body around the cluttered furniture to show each piece off to best advantage.

During her time working with Howard she had seen many wonderful pieces, had visited many stately homes and purchased deceased estates, but nothing in her experience came anywhere near what was in Jake's father's house. She'd completed enough courses by correspondence to recognise a genuine antique when she saw it and this house was practically filled floor to ceiling with them, most of them bordering on priceless.

It only begged the question why someone had collected such expensive showpieces when he'd clearly had no intention of ever showing them off. They were cheek by jowl in an old neglected house that needed more than a lick of paint on the outside and a great deal of it inside as well.

From the unfaded splendour of the furniture she could only assume the blinds at the windows had nearly always been kept down. She couldn't help thinking what sort of life Jake must have had as a young child in this mausoleum-like house. She couldn't imagine her little son lasting even a full minute without touching or breaking something valuable. She looked at a Prattware cat and wondered if Jake had ever broken anything in the boisterousness of youth. Lachlan had recently accidentally toppled over a vase at Howard's house and Marguerite Caule had torn strips off him, reducing him to tears even though the vase hadn't even been so much as chipped.

She gave an inward shudder and left the room.

The closed door of what used to be Jake's bedroom was three doors away down the hall. She looked at it for a long moment, wondering what secrets he kept locked there. She walked slowly towards the door, each of her footsteps making the floorboards creak as if they were warning her not to go any further. Jake had forbidden her to go in, telling her he kept it locked at all times, but she wouldn't be human or indeed even female if she didn't try the handle just the once…

It opened without a sound.

She stared at the open space before her for at least half a minute until the overwhelming temptation finally sent her feet forward, one after the other, until she was inside, the door as her hand left it, shifting soundlessly to a half-open position behind her.

It wasn't as dark as the rest of the rooms in the house. The blinds were not pulled all the way down and, although the sky outside was cloudy, enough light still came through for her to see the narrow single bed along one wall. Compared to the rest of the furniture in the house, Jake's bedroom was furnished roughly, almost cheaply. There was nothing of any significant value, that she could see. The wardrobe was little more than a chipboard affair and the chest of drawers not much better. There was a single mirror on the wall above the chest of drawers but it was cracked and crooked as if someone had bumped against it heavily but not bothered to straighten it again.

The bed was lumpy and looked uncomfortable, the ugly brown chenille spread bald in spots. The walls looked pock-marked, bits of poster glue still visible, although there was not a poster or photograph in sight. Again she thought of her childhood home with the walls covered with loving happy memories. Jake's childhood house was stripped of any such sentimentality. She had asked him once when they lived to-gether to show her a photo of himself as a child but he'd told her he hadn't bothered bringing any overseas with him. She had accepted his answer as reasonable and had thought nothing more about it. But now, in the aching emptiness of this room, she couldn't help wondering if anyone had ever taken one of him and cherished it the way her parents cherished the ones they had collected over the years.

There were no loving memories in this house.

The thought slipped into her head and once it took hold she couldn't erase it. The painful truth of it seemed to be seeping towards her, like a nasty stain that had been hidden for a long time but was now finally coming through the cracked paint on the walls to taint her with its dark shameful secret.

Jake had been abused by his father.

Her stomach clenched in anguish as the puzzle began to fall into sickening place. It all made sense now. No wonder he was getting rid of everything to do with his father. And no wonder he had never wanted children of his own.

Oh, Jake! Why didn't you tell me?

She looked again at the askew mirror on the wall and her stomach gave another painful lurch. Was that blood smeared in one corner?

Her eyes fell away from its mottled secrets and went to the chest of drawers beneath it. Almost of its own volition, her hand began to reach for the first drawer. She knew it was contravening Jake's rule but she had to find out what she could about his background. It was like a compulsion, an addiction she just had to feed, if only for the one time.

The drawer slid uneasily from its tracks as if it too was advising her against prying as the floorboards had seemed to do earlier, the scrape of rough-edged timber sounding like fingernails being dragged down the length of a chalk board.

She suppressed a tiny shiver and looked down at the odd socks tumbled in a heap, no two seemed to match or were even tucked together in the hope of being considered a pair. There was a bundle of underwear that looked faded and worn and a few unironed handkerchiefs not even folded.

The second drawer had a few old T-shirts, none of them ironed, only one or two folded haphazardly. A sweater was stuffed to one side, one of its exposed elbows showing a gaping hole.

Jeans were in the third drawer, only two pairs, both of them ragged and torn. She couldn't help a tiny smile. Both her sisters insisted on buying torn and ragged jeans; it was the fashion and they paid dearly for it, insisting they would *die* if anyone saw them in anything else.

She pushed against the drawer to shut it but it snagged and wouldn't close properly. She gave it another little shove but it refused to budge. She bent down and peered into the space between the second and third drawers but it was hard to see in the half light. She straightened and tugged the drawer right out of the chest in order to reinsert it, to check if anything was stuck behind.

A small package fell to the floor at her feet and, carefully sliding the drawer back into place, she bent down to retrieve it...

CHAPTER SIX

IT WAS an envelope, the edges well-worn as if it had been handled too many times. Ashleigh opened the flap and drew out the small wad of photographs it contained, her breath stalling in her throat as the first one appeared.

It was Jake as a small toddler and he looked exactly like Lachlan at the same age.

'I thought I told you this room was out of bounds.'

Ashleigh spun around so quickly she dropped the photographs, each of them fluttering to the floor around her quaking legs and feet.

'I...I...' She gave up on trying to apologise, knowing it was going to be impossible to get the words past the choking lump in her throat.

Jake moved into the room and she watched in a shocked silence as he retrieved the scattered photographs off the floor, slipping them back inside the old envelope and putting them to one side.

'There is nothing of value in this room.' He gave the room a sweeping scathing glance before his eyes turned back to hers. 'I told you before.'

She moistened her mouth, shifting from foot to foot, knowing he had every right to be angry with her for stepping across the boundary he had set down.

'You always were the curious little cat, weren't you?' he said, stepping towards her.

Ashleigh felt her breath hitch as he stopped just in front of her, not quite touching but close enough for her to feel the warmth of his body. It came towards her in waves, carrying with it the subtle scent of his essential maleness, his lemon-scented aftershave unable to totally disguise the fact that he'd been physically active at some point that morning. It was an intoxicating smell, suggestive of full-blooded male in his prime, testosterone pumped and charged, ready for action.

'The door…it wasn't locked…'

'It usually is, but I decided to trust you,' he said. 'But it seems I can no longer do so.'

She didn't know what to make of his expression. She didn't think he was angry with her but there was a hint of something indefinable in his gaze that unnerved her all the same.

'I was just checking…' she said lamely.

He gave a little snort of cynicism. 'I just bet you were.'

'I was!' she insisted. 'Was it my fault you left the door unlocked?'

'You didn't have to search through my things,' he pointed out.

'You haven't lived in this house for something like eighteen years,' she said. 'I'm surprised anything of yours is still here.'

He gave her an unreadable look. 'Quite frankly, so am I.'

She frowned at his words, her brain grappling with why his father had left things as they were. The room looked as if Jake had walked out of it all those years ago and yet it seemed as if nothing had been removed or changed since.

'Maybe he missed you,' she offered into the lengthy silence.

Jake's dark eyes hardened as they pinned hers. 'Yes, I suppose he did.'

She ached to ask why but the expression on his face warned her against it. Anger had suddenly tightened his jaw, sent fire to his eyes and tension to his hands as they fisted by his sides.

She couldn't hold his look. She turned and found herself looking at her own reflection in the cracked mirror on the wall. It was like looking at a stranger. Her blue eyes looked wild and agitated, her hair falling from the neat knot she had tied it in that morning, her cheeks flushed, her mouth trembling slightly.

She could see him just behind her. If she stepped back even half a step she would come into contact with the hard warmth of his very male body. Her workout in the gym that morning made her aware of her body in a way she had not been in years. She felt every used muscle, every single contraction reminding her of how she used to feel in his arms. Making love with Jake had been just like a heavy workout. He had been demanding and daring, taking her to the very limits of consciousness time after time until she hadn't known what was right and decent any more.

She met his eyes in the mirror and suppressed an inward shudder of reaction. Would she ever be able to look at him without feeling a rush of desire so strong it threatened to overturn every moral principle she had been taught to cling to?

She sucked in a breath as his hands came down on her shoulders, his eyes still locked on hers in the mirror. She did her best to control her reaction but the feel of his long fingers on her bare skin melted her resolve. She positively ached for him to slowly and sensually slide his hands down the length of her arms as he used to do, his fingers curling around the tender bones of her wrists in a hold that brooked no resistance. She wondered if he knew how he still affected her, that her heart was already racing at the solid presence of him standing so close behind her, the knowledge that in the past his hardened maleness, thick with desire, would be preparing to plunge between her legs and send every trace of gasping air out of her lungs.

'Y-you're touching me...' Her voice came out not much more than a croak.

'Mmm, so I am.' His hands moved slowly down her arms, his eyes never once leaving hers.

She moistened her parched lips when his fingers finally encircled her wrists, her breathing becoming ragged and uneven. 'Y-you're breaking the rules, Jake.'

'I know.' He gave her a lazy smile as his thumbs began a sensual stroking of the undersides of her wrists. 'But you broke my one and only rule and now I shall have to think of a suitable penalty.'

She wasn't sure if it was she who turned in his arms or if he turned her to face him, but suddenly she wasn't looking at his reflection in the mirror any more but into his darker than night gaze as it burned down into hers.

His body was too close.

She could feel the denim seam of the waistband of his jeans against her, and when his hands drew her even closer her stomach came into contact with his unmistakable arousal. No one else could make her feel this way. Her body remembered and hungered for what it had missed for so long.

When his mouth came down over hers a tiny involuntary whimper of pleasure escaped her already parted lips, and as his tongue began an arrogant and determined search for hers she gave no resistance but curled hers around his in a provocative dance which spoke of mutual blood-boiling desire.

Ashleigh vaguely registered the dart of lightning that suddenly lit the room and the distant sound of thunder, the low grumble not unlike the sounds coming from Jake's throat as he took the kiss even further, his body grinding against hers. She wound her arms around his neck, her fingers burrowing into his thick dark silky hair, her breasts tight with need as they were crushed against his chest.

Jake sucked on her bottom lip, a bone-melting act he'd perfected in the past, making her feel as if her body and mind were totally disconnected. She no longer felt like someone else's fiancé. She felt like Jake's lover, a lover who knew exactly how to please him. She remembered it all so well! How to make him groan with ecstasy as he spilled himself into her body, her mouth or wherever she chose to tempt him beyond the tight limits of his control.

Now she couldn't help relishing the feeling of power his reaction afforded her. She could sense his struggle to hold back as his tongue thrust back into her mouth, the sexy male rasp inciting her to give back even more. She bit down on his bottom lip, a tantalising little nip that made him growl deep in his throat. She wouldn't release him, supping on him as if she wanted to take him deep inside and never let him go.

She loved the feel of his hard mouth, the way his masculine stubble never seemed to be quite under smooth enough control, the rough scrape of skin against the softness of hers reminding her of all that was different between them.

How had she lived without his touch? This madness of blood racing through veins alight with passion, a frenzy of feeling that would not go away without the culmination of physical union.

And then only temporarily.

When she felt Jake's hands slide beneath her top she did nothing to stop him. She couldn't. Her breasts were aching too much for the cup of his warm hands, hands that in the past her too slim body hadn't quite been able to fill. But it did now.

Her flesh spilt into his hands as he released her simple bra, the stroke of his fingers over the tight buds of her nipples an almost unbearable pleasure. When he bent his head to place his hot mouth on her right nipple she nearly fainted with reaction, the slippery motion of his tongue stirring her into a madness of need that she knew had only one assuagement. He knew it too, for he did the same to her other breast, drawing little agonised gasping groans from her lips, her cheeks flushing with passion, her limbs weakening as she leant into his iron-strong hold.

He pressed her backwards until the backs of her knees came into contact with his narrow single bed. A distant corner of her conscience prodded her, reminding her of her commitment to Howard. But somehow when Jake's long strong body came down over hers and pinned her to the mattress, any notion of resistance disappeared on the tail end of a gasp as his thighs nudged between the quivering silk of hers.

'I have waited so long to do this,' Jake groaned as he lifted her skirt with impatient hands, his eyes like twin torches of fire as he looked down at her desire-flushed features. 'I have dreamt of it, ached for it, planned for it until I could think of nothing else.'

Planned for it? Ashleigh froze as his words sank in. She eased herself up on her elbows, dislodging his weight only because he hadn't expected it. 'What do you mean, *planned* for it?' she asked.

He began to press her back down but she pushed his hand away. 'No, Jake. Tell me what you mean.'

He gave her a frustrated look from beneath frowning brows. 'Do we have to talk *now?*'

'Yes.' She rolled off the bed and quickly rearranged her clothing with as much dignity as she could, and turned to face him determinedly. 'Tell me what you meant. Now.'

He drew in a harsh breath and got off the bed in a single movement, one of his hands marking a rough pathway through his hair. 'I have made no secret of my intention to see you again,' he said. 'I told you that the very first day.'

She gave him a reproachful glare. 'You also told me the following day that you had no intention of sleeping with me, or have you forgotten that little detail?'

His mouth curled up in one corner as he looked down at her. 'I was only responding to the invitation you've been sending out to me from the first moment we met in the hotel bar. You can deny it all you like, but you're as hungry for me as I am for you.'

'I. Am. Engaged.' She bit the words out with stiff force.

His cynical smile tilted even further. 'Just exactly who are you reminding of the fact, me or you?'

Ashleigh had never felt closer to violence in her entire life. Her hand twitched with the desire to take a swipe at the self-satisfied smirk on his darkly handsome face, and in the end only some tiny remnant of her conservative upbringing forestalled her.

She clenched her fists by her sides and berated him coldly. 'If you think you can replay our relationship just for the heck of it you're very much mistaken. I know what you're doing, Jake. As soon as you clean up this place you'll be back off to London or Paris or wherever you have some other stupid misguided woman waiting in vain for you to commit.'

'That has always been a sticking point with you, hasn't it?' he said, folding his arms in a casual unaffected pose. 'You don't think a relationship is genuine without some sort of formal commitment.'

She found it difficult to hold his very direct look but before she could think of a response he continued, 'Which kind of makes me wonder why you don't wear an engagement ring. Can't poor old Howard even rustle up a second-hand one for you?'

It was all she could do to keep her temper under control.

Rage fired in her blood until she could see tiny red spots of it before her eyes. She so wanted to let fly at him with every gram of bitterness she'd stored up over the years, but instead of a stream of invective coming out of her mouth when she finally opened it, to her utter shock, shame and embarrassment a choked sob came out instead.

Jake stared at her, his own mouth dropping open as she bent her head to her hands, her slim shoulders visibly shaking as she tried to cover the sounds of her distress.

He muttered one short sharp curse and reached for her, pulling her into the shield of his chest, one of his hands cupping the back of her silky head as he brought it down against his heart.

'I'm sorry.' He was surprised it hadn't physically hurt to articulate the words, especially as he'd never said them to anyone before.

She didn't answer other than to burrow a bit closer, but after a moment or two he could feel the dampness of her tears through his thin cotton T-shirt.

He couldn't remember ever seeing her cry before. He'd always secretly admired her for it, actually. His childhood had taught him that tears were for the weak and powerless; he'd disciplined himself not to cry from an early age and, no matter what treatment had been dished out to him, he had been determined not to let his emotions get out of control. He had gritted his teeth, sent his mind elsewhere, planned revenge and grimly stored his anger, and for the most part he'd succeeded.

The only time he'd failed was the day his father had told him his dog had been sent away to the country. Jake had only been about ten and the little fox-terrier cross had been a stray he'd brought home. Her excited yaps when he'd come home from school each day had been the highlight of his young life.

The *only* highlight.

No one else had ever looked that happy to see him since… well…maybe Ashleigh had in their early days together, her eyes brightening like stars as he'd walked in the door.

Ashleigh eased herself out from his hold and brushed at her eyes with the back of her hand, her other hand hunting for a much-needed tissue without success.

Jake reached past her and opened the top drawer of the chest of drawers and handed her one of the crumpled hand-kerchiefs. 'Here,' he said, his tone a little gruff, 'it's more or less clean but I'm afraid it's not ironed.'

'It doesn't matter,' she said, turning away to blow her nose rather noisily.

Jake watched her in silence, wishing he could think of something to say to take away the gaping wound of their past so they could start again. He knew he didn't really deserve the chance, but if he could just explain…

He wanted to change. He wanted to be the sort of man she needed, the solid dependable type, the sort of man who would be a brilliant father to the children he knew she wanted to have. But what guarantee could he give her that he wouldn't turn out just like his father? Things might be fine for a year or two, maybe even a little longer, but he knew the patterning of his childhood and the imprint of his genes would win in the end.

He'd read the statistics.

Like father like son.

There was no getting away from it.

He just couldn't risk it.

Ashleigh scrunched the used handkerchief into a ball in her hand and turned back to meet his gaze. 'I'm sorry about that…' She bit her lip ruefully. 'Not my usual style at all.'

He smiled. Not cynically. Not sneeringly, but sadly, his coal-black eyes gentle, the normally harsh lines of his mouth soft. 'No,' he agreed, 'but everyone has their limits, I guess.'

She lowered her gaze, concentrating on the round neckline

of his close-fitting T-shirt. 'I think it's this house…' She rubbed at her upper arms as if she was suddenly cold. 'It seems sort of…sort of miserable…and…well…sad.'

Jake privately marvelled at the depth of her insight, but if only she knew even half of it! The walls could tell her a tale or two, even the mirror behind her bore the scar of his final fight with his father. He'd been fully expecting to see his blood still splattered like ink drops all over it and the wall but apparently his father had decided to clean up his handiwork, although it looked as if he'd missed a bit in one corner.

He forced his thoughts away from the past and, reaching for the envelope he'd put aside earlier, sat on the bed and patted the space beside him, indicating for her to sit alongside. 'Hey, come here for a minute.'

He saw the suspicion in her blue eyes and held up his hands. 'No touching, OK?'

She came and sat on the bed beside him, her hands in her lap and her legs pressed together tightly.

He opened the envelope with careful, almost reverent fingers and Ashleigh found herself holding her breath as he took out the first photograph.

It was the photo she'd seen earlier. It was the spitting image of Lachlan at the age of eighteen months or so—the engaging smile, the too long limbs and the olive skin the sun had kissed where summer clothes hadn't covered.

She didn't know what to say, so said nothing.

'I was about a year and a half old, I think,' Jake said, turning over the photo to read something scrawled in pencil on the back. 'Yeah…'

'What does it say?' she asked.

He tucked the photo to the back of the pile, his expression giving little away. 'Not much. Stuff about what I was doing, words I was saying, that sort of thing. My mother must have written it.'

Ashleigh felt the stabbing pain of her guilt as she thought about the many photographs she had with Lachlan's early life documented similarly.

Jake took out the next photograph and handed it to her. She felt the warm brush of his fingers against hers but didn't pull away. She held the photograph with him, as if the weight of the memories it contained was too heavy for one hand.

It was a photograph of a small dog.

Ashleigh wished she had her sister Ellie's knowledge of canine breeds but, taking a wild guess, she thought it looked like a fox-terrier with a little bit of something else thrown in. It had a patch of black and tan over one cheeky bright intelligent eye and another two or three on its body, its long narrow snout looking as if it was perpetually smiling.

She glanced at him, their fingers still linked on the picture. 'Was this your dog?'

He nodded and shifted his gaze back to the photograph. She sensed rather than heard his sigh.

'What happened to him?' she asked after what seemed an interminable silence.

'Her,' he corrected, without looking up from the image.

Ashleigh held her breath, instinctively knowing more was to come. Exactly what, she didn't know, but for now it was comforting that he trusted her enough to show her some precious relics of his past. Somehow she knew he hadn't done this before.

With anyone.

Jake tucked the photograph behind the others and closed the envelope. 'I called her Patch. She followed me home from school one day when I was about eight or so.'

'How long did you have her?'

'A year or two.'

'She died?'

He met her gaze briefly before turning away. 'My father sent her to live in the country.'

Ashleigh felt her stomach clench with sympathy for the child he had been and the loss he must have felt. 'Why?'

He gave another small shrug. 'I must have done something to annoy him.' He pushed the envelope away and stood up. 'As punishments went it was probably the best he'd ever come up with, not that I ever let on, of course.'

Ashleigh could just imagine how stoical he had been. His chin stiff, no hint of a wobble even though inside his heart would have been breaking. Hadn't she seen it in Lachlan when Purdy, the family's ancient but much loved budgerigar, had died not that long ago?

'Did you ever get to visit her?' she asked.

'No.' The single word was delivered like a punctuation mark on the subject, effectively closing it.

'Can I see the rest of the photos?' she asked after another stretching silence.

He pushed the envelope into the top drawer of the chest of drawers by way of answer. Ashleigh looked at the stiff line of his back as it was turned towards her, somehow sensing he'd let her past a previously well-guarded barrier and was now regretting his brief lapse into sentimentality. She could almost see the words Keep Out written across his face as he turned to look at her.

'Maybe some other time.' He moved past her to the door and held it open for her. 'Don't let me keep you from your work.'

Ashleigh brushed past him with her head down, not sure she wanted him to see the disappointment in her eyes at his curt dismissal. He'd allowed her into his inner sanctum for a moment, had made himself vulnerable to her in a way she'd never experienced with him before. It made it extremely difficult to use her bitterness as a barrier to what she really felt for him. The feelings she'd locked away for years were creeping out, finding gaps in the fences she'd constructed around herself. Her love for Jake was like a robust climbing vine that refused to die no matter how hard it was pruned or poisoned.

Ashleigh went into the first room she came to rather than have Jake's gaze follow her down the length of the hall. It was a dining room, the long table set with an array of dusty crockery and china, instantly reminding her of Miss Havisham's abandoned wedding breakfast in Charles Dickens's *Great Expectations*.

She reached for the light switch and watched as the ornate crystal chandeliers overhead flickered once or twice as if deciding whether to make the effort to throw some light in the room or not. The delicate drape of spiders' webs only added to the Dickensian atmosphere. She gave herself a mental shake and stepped further into the room to reach for the nearest blind, but just as she took hold of the tasselled cord a big furry black spider tiptoed over the back of her hand.

It was probably her best-ever scream.

Her mother had always said that Ashleigh held the record in the Forrester family for the scream that could not only wake the dead but everybody sleeping this side of the Blue Mountains as well.

The door behind her crashed open so roughly that the delicate glassware on the dining room table shivered in reaction as Jake came bursting in.

'What happened?' He rushed to her, his hands grasping her upper arms as he looked down at her pale face in concern.

'Nothing…' She gave a shaky little laugh of embarrassment and moved out of his hold. 'It was a spider, that's all.'

He frowned. 'I didn't know you were scared of spiders.'

'I'm not.' She rubbed the back of her hand on her skirt. 'I just don't like them using me as a pedestrian crossing.'

He glanced at what she was doing with her hand and grimaced. 'Where is it now?' He swept his gaze across the window-frame before looking back at her. 'Do you want me to get rid of it for you?'

'It's probably long gone,' she said. 'I think I screamed it into the next century.'

He gave her one of his rare genuine smiles. 'I thought you'd seen a ghost. I had no idea anyone so small could scream so loudly.'

Small? One gym workout and he already thought she was smaller? Thank you, Mia!

'I've had a lot of practice over the years,' she said. 'Mia and Ellie and I used to have screaming competitions.'

'Your poor parents,' Jake commiserated wryly.

'Yes…' A small laugh bubbled from her lips before she could stop it. 'The police were called once. Apparently one of the neighbours thought someone was being murdered or tortured at the very least. You should have heard the lecture we got for…' Her words trailed away as she saw the expression on Jake's face. It had gone from mildly amused to mask-like, as if something she had said had upset him and he didn't want to let her see how much.

'Jake?' She looked at him questioningly, her hand reaching out to touch him gently on the arm.

He moved out of her reach and turned to raise the blind.

The angry black clouds had by now crept right over the garden, their threatening presence casting the room in menacing, creeping shadows. The flickering light bulbs in the chandelier over the table made one last effort to keep the shadows at bay before finally giving up as a flash of sky-splitting lightning came through the window, momentarily illuminating the whole room in a ghostly lucency. The boom of thunder was close on its heels, the ominous sound filling Ashleigh's ears.

'Are you afraid of storms?' Jake asked without turning to look at her.

'No… not really,' she said, waiting a few seconds before adding, 'are you?'

She watched as he turned to look at her, the eerie light of the morning storm casting his face into silhouette.

'I used to be,' he answered, his voice sounding as if it had come from a distant place. 'But I'm not anymore.'

She waited a heartbeat before asking, 'How did you overcome your fear?'

It seemed an age before he responded. Ashleigh felt the silence stretching to breaking-point, her mind already rehearsing various phrases to relieve it, when he suddenly spoke, shocking her into vocal muteness.

'My father always used nature to his advantage. If a storm was loud and ferocious enough it would screen his activities from the neighbours.' He gave her a soulless look. 'Of course none of the neighbours called the police. They thought the booms and crashes going on were simply the effects of the storm.'

Ashleigh felt a wave of nausea so strong she could barely stand up. How had Jake survived such a childhood? She almost felt ashamed of how normal and loving her background was. She had been nurtured, along with her sisters, like precious hothouse flowers, while Jake had been consistently, cruelly crushed underfoot like a noxious weed.

'Oh, Jake…' She breathed his name. 'Why didn't you tell me?'

He gave a rough sound that was somewhere between scorn and dismissal. 'I'm over it, Ashleigh. My father's dead and I have to move on. Storms are just storms to me now. They hold no other significance.'

For some reason which she couldn't quite explain, her gaze went to the scar above his right eye. The white jagged line interrupted the aristocratic arc of his eyebrow like a bulldozed fire trail through a forest.

'Your eye…' she said. 'You always said you got that scar in a fight.' She took an unsteady breath and continued. 'Your father did it, didn't he?'

Jake lifted a hand and fingered the scar as if to make sure it was still there. 'Yes,' he said. 'It was the last chance he got to carve his signature on me. I was two days off my sixteenth birthday. I left and swore I'd never see him again.'

'You kept your promise…' She said the words for him.

He gave her a proud defiant look. 'Yes. I never saw him alive again.'

'I wish you'd told me all of this when we…when we were together,' she said. 'It would have helped me to understand how you—'

His lip curled into one of his keep-away-from-me snarls. 'What good would it have done? You with your perfect little family, everyone chanting how much they love each other every night as the night closed in like in all of those stupid TV shows. Do you know anything about what really goes on behind closed doors? Do you even know what it is like to go without a meal?' he asked, his tone suddenly savage, like a cornered neglected dog which had known nothing but cruelty all its life. 'Do you know what it is like to dread coming home at the end of the school day, wondering what punishment was in store if you so much as made a floorboard creak or a door swing shut too loudly?'

Ashleigh's eyes watered and she bit her lip until she could taste the metallic bitterness of blood.

Jake slashed one of his hands through the air like a knife and continued bitterly. 'I had no respite. From the day my mother died when I was three I lived with a madman. Not a day went past when I didn't have fear turning my guts to gravy while he watched and waited, timing his next hit for maximum effect.' He strode to the window once more, the next flash of angry lightning outlining his tall body as he stared out at the garden.

Ashleigh wanted to say something but knew this was not her turn to speak. Jake had been silent for most of his life; it was his turn to talk, to get what he could out of his system and he had chosen her to be witness to it.

He gave a deep sigh and she heard him rub his face with one hand, the slight raspy sound making her weak with her need to go to him in comfort. How she wanted to wrap her arms around him, to press soft healing kisses on all the spots on his body where his father had kicked, punched or brutalised him.

It was almost impossible for her to imagine someone wanting to harm their own child. She thought of Lachlan and how she would gladly give her life for his, had in fact given up so much for him already and not once complained. How could Jake's father have been so heartless? What possible motive could he have had to inflict such unspeakable cruelty on a defenceless child?

Jake turned around to look at her, his expression bleak. 'For most of my life I have done everything possible not to imitate my father. My life's single goal has been to avoid turning into a clone of him.'

She drew in a shaky little breath, hardly able to believe she was finally witnessing the confession she had always longed to hear.

'He remarried more often than he changed his shirts,' he continued in the same flat tone. 'I had a procession of stepmothers come in and out of my life, each of whom left as soon as they found out the sort of man my father was. I decided marriage was never going to be an option for me in case I ended up the same way, leaving a trail of emotional and physical destruction in my wake as my father did.'

'He abused you…didn't he?' Her voice came out on a thin thread of sound.

Jake's eyes shifted away from hers, his back turned towards her as he raised the ragged blind and stared out of the window.

'Not sexually,' he answered after what seemed another interminable pause.

Ashleigh felt her tense shoulders sag with instant relief.

'But he did just about everything else.'

Her stomach clenched, her throat closing over. 'Oh, Jake…'

He turned back to face her, his expression rueful. 'Do you realise you are the first person I've ever told this to?'

'I—I am?'

He gave her a sad smile. 'Every single day we lived together I wanted to tell you, but I thought if I did you would run a mile in case I turned out just like him.'

'You could never be like him, Jake…'

He turned back to the window, effectively shutting her out again.

'I have to go away for a few days,' he said into the silence, his voice sounding gut-wrenchingly empty.

After another little silence he turned around to look at her, the storm raging outside his backdrop. 'I have some things to see to interstate and I won't be back before the weekend.'

'That's OK,' she said softly. 'I can continue with the assessment on my own. There are quite a few things I'll need to do some research on anyway in order to give you some idea of valuation.'

'I don't care what this stuff is worth; I just want it out of here,' he said.

Ashleigh watched as he strode out of the room, his eyes avoiding hers as if he didn't want her to see the residual pain reflected there.

She didn't need to see it, she thought sadly, as the door clicked shut behind him.

She could *feel* it for him.

CHAPTER SEVEN

'BUT I don't want to go to crèche!' Lachlan whined for the fifth time a few days later on the Friday morning.

Ashleigh's patience was wearing thin. She hadn't slept properly in days, unable to erase the images of Jake's haunted past from her mind. Each day she'd spent in the old house seemed to make it worse, especially as he wasn't coming back until Monday to break the long aching silences. She knew it was disloyal to Howard, but she missed seeing Jake, missed hearing him move about the house and garden. God help her, she even missed his snarls and scornful digs.

'You have to go, Lachlan,' she insisted, stuffing his lunch box in his backpack.

'But I want to come wif you!' His chin wobbled and his dark eyes moistened.

Ashleigh felt the strings on her heart tighten; her son's little speech impediment always returned in moments of stress. She put the backpack to one side and squatted down in front of him, holding his thin shoulders so that he had to look at her.

'What's wrong, darling? Is someone making you unhappy at crèche?'

He shook his head, his bottom lip extended in a pout.

She gently pushed on his lip with the tip of her finger. 'You'll

trip over that if you poke it out any further.' She gave him a smile
as his lip returned to base. 'Now, what's all this about?'

He shuffled from one foot to the other. 'I just want to be
wif you.'

Ashleigh sighed. 'Darling, you know I have to work. We
can't live with Granny and Grandad for ever. They need time
alone and we need to have our own place too. As soon as
Howard and I get married…' She found it strange saying the
words and secretly wished she could take them back.

'Can I have a dog when we move to Uncle Howard's?'
Lachlan asked hopefully.

She forced her attention back to her son. His desire for a
dog had been so strong but her mother's allergy to cat and
dog hair had prevented it happening. However, Howard's
home with its pristine family heirloom décor was hardly the
family home a playful puppy would be welcomed into. She
could almost see Marguerite Caule's look of horrified distaste
at the first set of muddy pawprints on the pristine white carpet
or one of the linen-covered sofas.

'We'll see,' she said and straightened.

'We'll see means no,' Lachlan said with the sort of acuity
that marked him as Jake's son if nothing else. 'You always
say that, but it doesn't mean yes.'

She sighed and, zipping up his backpack, reached for his
hand. 'Come on, I'm late as it is.'

'I'm not going to crèche.' He snatched his hand away.

'Lachlan, I will not tolerate this from you,' she said
through tight lips. 'I have to go to…to that house I'm working
at and I have to leave now.'

'Take me to the house!' he begged. 'I'll be good. I won't
touch anyfing.'

Ashleigh closed her eyes as she pinched the bridge of
her nose.

Today of all days, she winced in frustration. Her mother

was out at a fundraising breakfast and wouldn't be back for hours. It was her father's annual heart check-up appointment in town and he'd left early to avoid the traffic and Mia had gone to an audition straight from the gym. Ellie, her last hope, hadn't come home yet from an all night sleep-in-the-park-for-homeless-dogs public awareness stunt that would probably see her on the front page of the morning's paper. It had happened before.

She let out her breath in a whoosh of tired resignation. 'All right, just this once. But if you so much as touch anything or break anything I won't let you watch *The Wiggles* or *Playschool* for a week.'

'Thank you, Mummy!' Lachlan rushed at her and buried himself against her, his arms around her waist, his cheek pressed to her stomach.

She eased him away to quickly scrawl a note for her mother who usually picked Lachlan up from the crèche on Friday afternoons to tell her about the change of plan.

'I love you, Mummy,' Lachlan said as she stuck the note on the fridge with a magnet.

'I love you, too, baby, but you're getting too big for pulling this sort of stunt.'

'What's a stunt?'

She tucked his hand in hers and shouldered open the door. 'Come on, I'll tell you in the car.'

Ashleigh was surprised and more than a little proud of the way Lachlan behaved at Jake's house. He had played quietly by her side as she worked in the library, never once complaining about being bored. He wheeled his little collection of toy cars across the floor, parking them in neat little rows on the squares on the Bakhtiari carpet with meticulous precision.

She knew she was taking a risk having him with her but

couldn't help feeling it had been worth it to see the simple joy on his little face every time she looked down at him.

She knew she was no different from every other working single mother, so often torn between the necessities to provide a reasonable living whilst allowing adequate time to nurture the child she'd brought into the world, but it still pained her to think how short-changed Lachlan was. Of late he'd been increasingly unsettled and clingy and she felt it was her fault. She'd thought her engagement to Howard would have offered him a bit more security but, while he liked Howard, she knew Marguerite intimidated him, although he did his very best not to show it.

'Can I go out into the garden for a while?' Lachlan got up from the floor with his little cars tucked into the old lunch-box container he kept them in, his dark eyes bright with hope.

Ashleigh pursed her lips as she thought about it. The garden, though large, was enclosed and the neighbourhood very quiet. The sun was shining, which it hadn't done properly in days, and she knew that—like most little boys his age—he needed lots of exercise and space.

'As long as you promise not to go through the side gate to the front; I can check on you while I'm working in this part of the house.'

'I promise,' he said solemnly.

A smile found its way to Ashleigh's mouth and she reached out a hand and ruffled his dark hair. 'Thanks for being so good this morning. It's really nice to have some company in this big old house.'

'Who lives here, Mummy?' Lachlan asked.

'No one at the moment,' she answered, fiddling with a gold shield-shaped bloodstone opening seal. 'The person who used to live here has…gone.'

'Did they die?'

It occurred to Ashleigh at that point that Lachlan had recently lost a blood relative, his paternal grandfather. It seemed unfair not to be able to tell her son who had actually lived in this house, when if things had been different he might have visited like any other grandson would have done, maybe even inherited some of the priceless pieces she was documenting.

But telling Lachlan would mean having to reveal the truth to Jake.

She wasn't ready to tell him and, given what she'd heard earlier that week about his childhood, Jake was nowhere near ready to hear.

'An old man used to live here,' she said.

'All by himself?' Lachlan asked, giving the imposing library a sweeping glance, his eyes wide with amazement.

'Yes…but a long time ago he used to live here with someone.'

'Who was it?' Lachlan's voice dropped, the sibilance of his childish whisper making Ashleigh feel slightly spooked.

'His…son.'

'Didn't he have a mummy too?'

'Yes…but she…she went away.' Ashleigh could see the stricken look come into Lachlan's eyes and wished she hadn't allowed the conversation to get to that point. As a child a few months off turning four who had grown up thus far without a father, his very worst nightmare was to have something take his mother away as well. She had always done her best to reassure him but still his fear lingered. She could see it in the way he looked at her at times, a wavering nervousness in his dark brown gaze, as if he wasn't sure if he would ever see her again once she walked out of the door.

She bent down and, tipping up his chin, pressed a soft kiss to the end of his nose. 'Why don't you go and explore the garden and in five minutes I'll join you. I'll bring out a drink and some fruit just like they do at crèche.'

His small smile brightened his features but did nothing to remove the shadow of uncertainty in his eyes. 'OK.'

She took his hand and led him back through the house to the back door, watching as he went down the steps with his car collection tucked under one small arm. He went straight to the elm tree, she noticed. The leafy shade was certainly an attraction on such a warm morning but she couldn't help wondering if it was somehow genetic.

She waited for a while, watching him set out his array of cars on the patches of earth where the lawn had grown thread-bare, parking each of them neatly before selecting one to drive up and down the exposed tree root nearest him.

A pair of noisy currawongs passed overhead and a light warm breeze stirred the leaves of the old elm, making each one shiver.

'I'll be out to check on you in five minutes, poppet,' she called out to him.

He didn't answer, which in a way reassured her. He was happy playing under the tree with the sounds of the birds to keep him company.

After being in the outdoor sunshine it took a moment for Ashleigh's eyes to adjust when she went back to the library. She took a few photos of some Tunbridge Ware book slides and stands and wrote a few notes about each, unconsciously gnawing the end of her pen as her thoughts gradually drifted to Jake.

She wondered where he was and who he was seeing interstate. She drew in a painful breath as she thought of him with another lover. Over the years she'd forced herself not to think of him in the arms of other women and mostly she'd been successful. She'd been too busy looking after his little son to torture herself with images of leggy blondes, racy redheads or brunettes with the sort of assets that drew men like bees to a paddock full of pollen.

'You look pensive,' Jake's deep voice said from the door of the library.

Ashleigh nearly swallowed the pen she had in her mouth

as she spun around in shock. 'What are you doing here?' she gasped, the pen falling from her fingers.

He eased himself away from the door frame where he'd been leaning and came towards her, stooping to pick up the pen and handing it to her with a quirk of one dark satirical brow. 'My business was dealt with a whole lot earlier than I expected,' he said. 'I thought I'd surprise you.'

You certainly did that, she mused, even as her stomach rolled over at the thought of him taking a look out of the library window. One look and she would have hell to pay.

She forced her features into impassivity. 'I didn't hear you come in… Which door did you use?'

'The front door,' he answered as he picked up a Tunbridge Ware bookmark and began to turn it over in his hands.

Ashleigh edged towards the window, waiting until she was sure Jake was looking elsewhere before quickly checking on Lachlan. Her heart gave an extra beat when she couldn't see him under the tree. She glanced back at Jake but he appeared to be absorbed in the bookmark. Checking the elm tree once more, she found her son had come back into view. Her heart's pace had only just settled down again as she turned back to look at Jake.

He was watching her steadily, his dark intelligent gaze securing hers.

'So…' She forcibly relaxed her shoulders, a tight smile stretching her mouth as her heart began its rollercoaster run again. 'How was your business trip?'

'It was nothing out of the ordinary,' he responded, his eyes never once moving away from hers. 'How have you been while I've been away?'

'Me?' It came out like a squeak and she hastily cleared her throat and began again. 'I mean…I'm fine. Great, been to the gym and feeling pretty fit and…' She couldn't finish the sentence under his probing gaze. She was rambling but she knew that if she didn't go out to Lachlan soon he would come in to her. She didn't know which would be worse. Maybe she should just come right out and tell Jake now before he set eyes on Lachlan. It wasn't much of a warning for him, but what else could she do?

She straightened her spine and faced him squarely. 'Jake… I have something to tell you that…' She took a much needed breath and continued. '…that I should have told you before, but I just felt it was never the right time, and—'

'Mummee!' A child's voice rang out from the back of the house, closely followed by the sound of little footsteps running down the hall.

Ashleigh swallowed painfully as her son came rushing into the room, her breath stopping completely when he cannoned into Jake's long legs encased in dark trousers.

She watched in stricken silence as Jake's hands steadied Lachlan, his touch gentle but sure as he looked down at the small face staring up at him.

'J-Jake, this is Lachlan,' she said in a voice she hardly recognised as coming from her own mouth. 'Lachlan, this is…Jake.'

Lachlan, with the impulsiveness of youth on his side, got in first. 'Are you the boy who used to live here a long time ago?'

Jake stared down at the little child in front of him for what seemed like endless minutes until he registered that the boy had spoken to him. 'Yes…I am,' he said, hoping his tone wasn't showing how shell-shocked he felt.

Ashleigh had a child.

The child she'd always wanted.

The child he wouldn't give her, *refused* to give her.

He couldn't look at her. He knew if he did she would see his disappointment, his *unjustified* disappointment.

So she'd had Howard's child.

He assumed it was Howard's, although the child in front of him certainly didn't look much like Ashleigh's fiancé, he had to admit. The sick irony of it was that the kid looked more like him. Once the thought was there it tried to take hold but he just as quickly dismissed it, although it surprised him how much it hurt to let it go.

There was no way that kid could have been his. He'd watched Ashleigh take her pills every day; it had been part of their daily ritual. *He* had made it a part of it. She'd never missed a dose and if she had he would have insisted on using an alternative until things were safe.

It was hard to assess the kid's exact age. He'd deliberately avoided everything to do with children for most of his adult life and had very little idea of what age went with what stage in a child's life. On what limited knowledge he had, he thought the boy might have been about three and a half, which meant Ashleigh had dived pretty quickly into Howard Caule's bed, but then, hadn't she done the same with him?

The prospect of fathering a child had always terrified him. He had become almost paranoid about it. The thought of spreading his father's genes to the next generation had been too much for him to bear. How could he ever forgive himself if he turned on his own child the way his father had done to him? Parenting wasn't an easy task. How soon would it have been before a light tap of reproof became a closed-fist punch? How quickly would his gentle chastising tone have turned into full-blown self-esteem eroding castigation? How many unspeakable hurts would he have inflicted before the child was damaged beyond repair?

Nothing had ever been able to convince him it would be desirable to father a child, and yet one look at Ashleigh's little son had rocked his conviction as only flesh and blood reality could do. She'd had another man's child because he had been too much of a coward to confront his past and deal with it appropriately.

A burning pain knifed through him as a sudden flood of self-doubt assailed him. But what if he *hadn't* turned out like his father? What if, in spite of all that had been done to him, he could have rewritten the past and become a wonderful father, the sort of father he had longed for all his life? One who would listen to the childish insecurities that had plagued him, especially after his mother had died. Who would have listened and comforted him instead of berating him and punishing for simply being a lost, lonely little boy.

Other people had difficult backgrounds; there was hardly a person alive who didn't have some axe to grind about their past. Why had he let his take over his life and destroy his one chance at happiness? His father had been violent and cruel and totally unworthy of the role of parent, but in the end the person who had hurt Jake the most had been himself. When Ashleigh had walked out of his life four and a half years ago he had done absolutely nothing to stop her. Instead he had stood before her, stiff and uncommunicative, as she accused him of being unfaithful after she'd mistakenly read one of his e-mails about his recent trip to Paris. He could have told her then and there the real reason for his weekend away but he hadn't, for it would have meant revealing the filthy shame of his past to her. In the end his pride had not been able to stretch quite that far.

'I was going to tell you…' Ashleigh said, taking Lachlan's hand in hers and drawing him close to her.

Jake saw the way the child's eyes were watching him, the sombre depths quietly assessing him. It unnerved him a bit to have a kid so young look at him so intently, as if he were searching for something he'd been looking for a long time.

'It's none of my business,' he said, wishing his tone had sounded a little more detached.

Ashleigh had been waiting for the bomb to drop and found it hard to grasp the context of his words for a moment. She studied his expression and nervously disguised a swallow as his eyes went to Lachlan before returning to hers.

'I know it's probably very sexist of me, but it sure didn't take you long to replace me, did it?' he said.

It took her a nanosecond to get his meaning but she didn't know whether to be relieved or infuriated. Couldn't he see his own likeness standing before him in miniature form?

'I don't think this is a conversation we should be having at this time,' she said, indicating her son by her side with a pointed look.

'You're right,' Jake agreed.

There was a tense little silence. Ashleigh hunted her brain for something to fill it but nothing she wanted to say was suitable with her young son standing pressed to her side, facing his father for the very first time.

She wanted to blame someone.

She wanted to pin the responsibility for this situation on her mother for having a prior commitment, on her father for having a heart condition that needed regular monitoring, on her sister Mia for having an audition and Ellie for having a social conscience that was too big for her. If any of them had been free she wouldn't be standing in front of Jake now with his son, with a chasm of misunderstanding and bitterness separating them.

But in the end she knew there was no one to blame but herself. She should have told Jake four and a half years ago, given him the choice whether to be involved in his child's life or not.

Her mother was right. Even if he had pressed her to have a termination, the final decision would surely have been hers. She had thought she was being strong by walking away but, looking back with the wisdom of hindsight, she had to concede that she'd taken the weakling's way out. She had run for cover instead of facing life head on.

She turned to Lachlan, schooling her features into a serenity she was far from feeling. 'Poppet, why don't you go back out to the garden and we'll join you in a few minutes?'

Lachlan slipped his hand out of hers and scampered away without a single word of protest. He gave one last look over his shoulder before his footsteps sounded out down the hall as he made his way to the back door leading out to the garden.

This time the silence was excruciating.

Ashleigh felt each and every one of its invisible tentacles reaching out to squeeze something out of her but her throat had closed over as soon as Jake's eyes came back to hers.

'He doesn't look much like Howard,' he commented.

'That's because he's not Howard's son.'

'You surprise me.' The cynical smile reappeared. 'I didn't think you were the sleep-around type.'

'I had a very good teacher,' she returned, marginally satisfied when his smile tightened into something else entirely.

'How old is he?' he asked after another tense moment or two.

'Why do you ask?'

He shrugged one shoulder. 'Isn't it the usual question to ask?'

'As you said earlier, it's none of your business.'

'Maybe, but I'd still like to know,' he said.

'Why?'

It seemed an age before he answered.

'Because I need to be absolutely sure he's not mine.' He scraped a hand through his hair and added, 'You would have told me if he was, wouldn't you?'

It was all Ashleigh could do to hold his penetrating gaze. She felt herself squirming under the weight of its probe, the burden of her secret causing her a pain so intense she could scarcely draw in a breath.

'You can take a paternity test, if you'd like,' she said, taking a risk she wasn't sure would pay off. 'Then you can be absolutely sure.'

He gave her a long contemplative look before asking, 'Are you in any doubt of who the child's father is?'

'No,' she answered evenly. 'No, I know exactly who the father is.'

Jake moved away and went to the window she'd guarded so assiduously earlier. 'It was the one thing I could never give you, Ashleigh,' he said with his back still towards her. 'I told you that from day one.'

'I know…'

'I just couldn't risk it,' he said. He took a deep breath and added, 'My father…'

She bit her lip as she heard the slight catch in his voice, knowing how difficult this was for him.

'My father suffered from a rare but devastating personality disorder,' he said heavily. 'It's known to be genetic.'

'I understand…'

Jake squeezed his eyes shut, trying to block out the vision of Ashleigh's child playing underneath the tree he'd spent most of his own childhood sheltering beneath or in.

'No, you can't possibly understand,' he bit out, turning around to face her. 'Do you think I've wanted to have this burden all my life? I wish I could walk away from it, be a normal person for once instead of having to guard myself from having a re-run of my childhood played out in front of me every day.'

'I'm sorry…' She lowered her eyes from the fire of his, unable to withstand the pain reflected in his tortured gaze.

'But I couldn't risk it,' he went on. 'I couldn't put that intolerable burden on to another person. Not you, or whatever children we might have produced. My father was a madman who could switch at any moment. I'd rather die than have any child of mine suffer what I suffered.'

'But it might have skipped a generation…' she offered in vain hope.

'And then what?' His eyes burned into hers. 'I would have to watch it played out in the next or even the one after that but have no control over it whatsoever.' His expression grew embittered as he continued, 'How could I do that and live with myself?'

Ashleigh swallowed painfully. The burden of truth was almost more than she could bear but she knew she couldn't tell him about Lachlan's true parentage now. It would totally destroy him.

She watched as he sent his hand through his hair, his eyes losing their heat to grow dull and soulless as he turned to stare out of the window, the wall of his back like an impenetrable barrier.

'You don't know how much I've always envied you, Ashleigh,' he said after another long moment of silence. 'You have the sort of background that in fact most people today would envy. You have two parents who quite clearly love each other and have done so for many years exclusively, two sisters who adore you and not a trace of ill feeling to cast a shadow over the last twenty-odd years you've spent being a family.' He turned and looked at her, his expression grim. 'I'm sorry for what I couldn't give you, Ashleigh. If it's any comfort to your ego, I was tempted. Damn tempted. More tempted than I'd ever been previously and certainly more tempted than any time since.'

'Thank you...' she somehow managed to say, her eyes moving away from the steady surveillance of his.

She heard him give one of his trademark humourless grunts of laughter.

'Aren't you going to ask me how many lovers I've had over the years? Isn't that what most women would have asked by now?'

'I'm not interested,' she answered.

'How many lovers have you had?' he asked.

'I told you before, it's none of your business.'

'Well…' He stroked the line of his jaw for a moment, the raspy sound of his fingers on his unshaven skin making Ashleigh's toes curl involuntarily. 'One has to assume there have been at least two. Your son's father for one and then, of course, there's dear old Howard.'

Ashleigh felt increasingly uncomfortable under his lazy scrutiny. She kept her eyes averted in case he caught even a trace of the hunger she knew was there. She could feel it. It crawled beneath the surface of her skin, looking for a way out. Even her fingertips twitched with the need to feel his flesh under them once more. Behind the shield of her bra she could feel the heavy weight of her breasts secretly aching for the heat and fire of his mouth and tongue, and her legs were beginning to tremble with the effort of keeping her upright when all they wanted was to collapse so her body could cling to the strength and power of his.

'Tell me, Ashleigh.' Jake's voice was a deep velvet caress across her too sensitive skin. 'Does Howard make you scream the way I used to?'

She stared at him speechlessly, hot colour storming into her cheeks, her hands clenching into fists by her sides.

'How dare you ask such a thing?' she spat at him furiously.

His lip curled. 'You find my question offensive?'

She sent him a heated glare. 'Everything about you is offensive, Jake. You might think handing over your father's goods for free gives you automatic licence to offend me at every opportunity, but I won't allow you to speak to me that way.'

'It's a perfectly reasonable question, Ashleigh,' he said. 'You and I did, after all, have something pretty special going on there for a couple of years way back then. I was just wondering, as any other man would, if your future husband comes up to scratch in the sack.'

She folded her arms and set her mouth. 'Unlike you, Jake Marriott, Howard treats me with a little more respect.'

'You mean he hasn't had you up against the kitchen bench with your knickers around your ankles?' he asked with a sardonic gleam in his dark eyes. 'Or what about the lounge room floor with all the curtains opened? Has he done you there? Or what about the—'

'Stop it!' She flew at him in outrage, her hands flying at his face to stop the stream of words that shamed her cruelly. 'Stop it!'

Jake caught her flailing arms with consummate ease and pulled her roughly into his embrace, his mouth crashing down on hers smothering her protests, her cries, even her soft gasp of pleasure…

His tongue slid along the surface of hers, enticing it into a sensuous, dangerous, tempting dance that sent the blood instantly roaring through her veins, the rush of it making her head swim with uncontrollable need—a need that had lain hidden and dampened down for far too long.

Ashleigh vaguely registered the sound of movement in the hall, but was too far gone with the sensations of Jake's commanding kiss to break away from his iron hold.

So what if Lachlan came in and found her kissing Jake as if there was no tomorrow? The truth was that there was no tomorrow for her and Jake, and this kiss would very probably have to last a lifetime.

But in the end it wasn't Lachlan's voice that had her springing from Jake's arms in heart-stopping shock.

It was her sister's.

CHAPTER EIGHT

'ASHLEIGH, I just thought I'd let you know—' Ellie pulled up short when she came across her sister's stricken look '—that Mum couldn't make it to pick up Lachlan so...so I decided to come and take him off your hands.' She pointed in the general direction of the front door. 'I did try and knock but there was...no answer...'

Jake let his arms fall from Ashleigh and greeted Ellie with his customary somewhat detached politeness.

'Hello, Ellie.' He brushed her cheek briefly with a kiss. 'You're looking...er...very grown up.'

Ashleigh felt like groaning at his understatement. Ellie had the sort of figure that turned heads, male and female, her most attractive feature, however, being that she seemed totally unaware of how gorgeous she looked.

'Hi, Jake!' Ellie beamed up at him engagingly. 'You're looking pretty good yourself.' She glanced about the room and added, 'Wow, this sure is some mansion.' She turned back to look at him. 'I didn't know you had a thing for antiques.'

'I don't,' Jake answered. 'Ashleigh is helping me sort through everything.'

Ashleigh wanted the floor to open up and leave her to the spiders under the house's foundations. Surely it would be bet-

ter than facing the knowing wink of her cheeky younger
sister, who was quite obviously speculating on the interest-
ing little tableau she'd just burst in on.

Ashleigh knew for a fact that Jake certainly wasn't suffer-
ing any embarrassment over it. She caught the tail-end of his
glinting look, his dark eyes holding an unmistakable promise
to finish what he'd started as soon as they were alone, rules
or no rules.

'Ashleigh will do a fine job, I'm sure, won't you, Ash?'
Ellie grinned. 'She'll have all your most valuable assets in
her hot little hands in no time.'

Ashleigh threw her a fulminating look but just then
Lachlan's footsteps could be heard coming along the hall.

'Auntie Ellie!' Lachlan came bounding in, instantly throwing his arms around Ellie's middle and squeezing tightly.

'Hi there, champ.' Ellie hugged him back and then bent
down to kiss the tip of his nose, 'How did you get out of going
to crèche, you monstrous little rascal?'

'I wanted to be with Mummy,' Lachlan answered, his
cheeks tinged with pink as he lowered his eyes.

Ellie straightened and, giving his hair a quick ruffle, kept
her hand on his little head as she turned to face her sister. 'I
saw your note so I thought I would come instead. I took the
bus so it will be a bit of a trek back, but Mum met up with an
old school friend. I thought it best if I left her to catch up over
a long lunch. Besides…' She tucked her spare hand into her
torn jeans pocket and tilted her platinum blonde head at Jake.
'I wanted to check out what Jake thought of his son now that
he's finally met him.'

Ashleigh felt every drop of blood in her veins come to a
screeching, screaming halt. She even wondered if she was
going to faint. She actually considered feigning it to get out
of the way of the shockwaves of the bomb Ellie had unthink-
ingly just delivered.

Six sickening heartbeats of silence thrummed in her ears as she forced herself to look at Jake standing stiffly beside her.

'*My son?*' Jake stared at Ellie in stupefaction.

Ashleigh saw the up and down movement of her sister's throat as she gradually realised the mistake she'd just made.

'I—I thought you knew…' Ellie turned to Ashleigh for help but her older sister's expression was ashen, the line of her mouth tight with tension. She swivelled back to Jake's burning gaze. 'I kind of figured that since Lachlan was here at your house…' Her words trailed off, her eyes flickering nervously between the two adults. 'I sort of thought…she must have told you by now…'

'Mummy?' Lachlan piped up, his childish innocence a blessed relief in the tense atmosphere. 'Can I show Auntie Ellie the garage for my cars I made under the tree?'

Ashleigh gave herself a mental shake. 'Sure, baby, take her outside and show her what you've been up to.'

'Come on, Auntie Ellie.' Lachlan took Ellie's hand and tugged it towards the door. 'I made a garage out of sticks and a driveway and a real race track. Do you want to see?'

'I can hardly wait,' Ellie said, meaning it, and giving her sister one last please-forgive-me glance, closed the door firmly behind them.

As silences between them went, this one had to be the worst one she'd ever experienced, Ashleigh thought as she dragged her gaze back to the minefield of Jake's.

'My son?' He almost barked the words at her.

She closed her eyes on the hatred she could see in his eyes.

'*My son?*' he asked again, his tone making her eyes spring open in alarm. 'You calculating, lying, deceitful little bitch! How could you do this to me?'

Ashleigh had no defence. She felt crushed by his anger, totally disarmed by his pain, not one word of excuse making it past the scrambled disorder of her brain.

He swung away from her, his movements agitated and jerky as if he didn't trust himself not to shake her senseless.

She watched in silent anguish as his hand scored his hair, the long fingers separating the silky strands like vicious knives.

'I can't believe you did this to me,' he said. 'I told you from day one this must never happen.' He swung back to glare at her. 'Did you do it deliberately? To force me into something I've been avoiding for all of my god-damned life?'

'I didn't do it deliberately,' she said evenly, surprised her voice came out at all.

His heavy frown took over his entire face. 'You were on the pill, for Christ's sake!'

'I know…' She bit her lip. 'I had a stomach bug when you were in New York that time…I didn't think…I thought it would be all right…'

'Why didn't you tell me, for God's sake?'

She stared at him, a slow-burning anger coming to her defence at long last. 'How could I possibly tell you? You would have promptly escorted me off to the nearest abortion clinic!'

He opened his mouth to say something but nothing came out.

'You were always so adamant about no kids, no pets and no permanent ties,' she went on when he didn't speak. 'How was I supposed to deal with something like an unexpected pregnancy? I was just twenty years old, I was living in another country away from the security I'd taken for granted for most of my life, living with a man who had no time for sentimentality or indeed any of the ethics that had been drummed into me from the day I was born. How was I supposed to cope with such a heart-wrenching situation?' She drew in a ragged breath. 'For all I knew, you would have had me off to the nearest facility to get rid of "my mistake" before I could even think of an alternative. I wanted time to think of an alternative…'

'What sort of alternative were you thinking of?' he asked after a stiff pause.

She met his eyes for a brief moment. 'I couldn't face… getting rid of it…' She turned away and examined her hands. 'I considered adoption, but having seen Ellie go through the heartache of wondering whether to seek out her blood relatives or not, I just couldn't do it. I knew I would spend the rest of my life wondering what my child was doing. Whether his new parents would love him the way I loved him…whether he was happy…' She lifted her head and gave him an agonised look and continued. 'I knew that on his birth date for the rest of my life I would wonder… I would ache… I would want to know how he was… I couldn't go through with it. I had to have him. I had no other choice.'

She stared back down at the tight knot of her hands. 'I knew you wouldn't want to know about his existence, so I decided to go it alone. I knew it wouldn't be easy but my family have been wonderful. They love Lachlan so much…I can't imagine life without him now.'

Jake turned away, not sure he could cope with Ashleigh seeing how seriously he was affected.

A son!

His son!

His father's grandson…

His stomach churned with fear. This is what he had spent his lifetime avoiding and now here it was, inescapable. Ashleigh had given birth to his child without his permission and now he had to somehow deal with it.

'I want a paternity test,' he said. 'I want it done immediately and if you don't agree I'll engage legal help to bring it about.'

Ashleigh felt another corner of her heart break.

'If that's what you need I won't stop you.'

'I want it done,' he said, hating himself for saying it. 'I want it done so at least I know where I stand.'

'I don't want anything from you,' she said. 'I've never wanted anything from you. That's why I didn't tell you. I couldn't bear the thought of you thinking of me as some sort of grasping woman who wanted their pound of flesh on top of everything else.'

'Were you ever going to tell me?'

His words dropped into the silence like a bucket of ice-cold water on flames.

She seemed to have trouble meeting his eyes. He wasn't sure what to make of it but he assumed in the end it was guilt. Her shoulders were slumped, her head bowed, her hands twisting in front of her.

'Answer me, damn you!' he growled. 'Were you ever going to tell me?'

She lifted her head, her eyes glazed with moisture.

'I thought about telling you that first night…at the bar…' Her teeth caught her bottom lip for a moment before she continued raggedly. 'But you were so arrogant about insisting on seeing me again, as if I'd had no life of my own since we broke up. It didn't seem the right atmosphere to inform you of…of Lachlan's existence.'

Jake turned away from her, his back rigid with tension as he paced the floor a couple of times.

He couldn't take it in.

He tried to replay their conversation at the hotel bar, to see if there had been any hint of her well-kept secret, but as far as he could recall she had only met him under sufferance and had given every appearance of being immensely relieved to escape as soon as she possibly could.

'Jake, please believe me,' she appealed to him, her voice cracking under the pressure. 'I wanted to tell you so many times but you seemed so out of reach. And when you finally told me about your father I knew that if I told you it would only cause more hurt.'

'Hurt?' He swung back to glare at her. 'Do you have any idea of what you've done? How much you have hurt me by this?'

She tried her best to hold his fiery look but inside she felt herself falling apart, piece by piece.

'I know it seems wrong now but I thought I was doing the right thing at the time,' she said. 'I didn't want an innocent child to suffer just because his father didn't want to be a father. I thought I'd do my best…bring him up to be a good man and one day…'

Jake slammed his hand down on the nearest surface, the crash of flesh on old wood jarring her already overstretched nerves.

'Don't you see, Ashleigh? If things were different I would have gladly embraced fatherhood.' One of his hands moved over his face in a rubbing motion before he continued, his eyes dark with immeasurable pain. 'If I didn't have the sort of gene pool I have, do you not think I wouldn't have wanted a son, a daughter, maybe even several?'

She choked back a sob without answering.

He gave a serrated sigh and continued. 'I have spent my life avoiding exactly this sort of situation. I even went as far as insisting on a vasectomy but I couldn't find a surgeon who would willingly perform it on a man in his early thirties, let alone when I was in my twenties, especially a man who supposedly hadn't yet fathered a child.'

'I'm so sorry…'

He turned to look at her. 'Does your fiancé know I'm the boy's father?'

Ashleigh raised her eyes to his, her head set at a proud angle. 'His name is Lachlan. I would prefer it if you would refer to him as such instead of as "the boy".'

'Pardon me for being a bit out of touch with his name,' he shot back bitterly. 'I have only just been informed of his existence. I don't even know his birth date.'

'Christmas Eve,' she answered without hesitation.

Ashleigh could see him do the mental arithmetic and silently prepared herself for the fallout.

'You were almost *four months pregnant* when you left me?' he gasped incredulously.

She hitched up her chin even more defiantly. 'It wasn't as if you would have noticed. You were no doubt too busy with one of your other international fill-ins. Who was it now…Sigrid?'

He lowered his gaze a fraction. 'I wasn't unfaithful to you that weekend.'

'Why should I believe you?' she asked. 'I read her e-mails, don't forget. She said how much she was looking forward to seeing you, how much she had enjoyed meeting you that first time and how she hoped your "association" with her would continue for a long time.'

Jake closed his eyes in frustration and turned away, his hands clenched by his sides as he bit out, 'She means nothing to me. Absolutely nothing.'

'That's the whole point, isn't it, Jake?' she said. 'No one ever means anything to you. You won't allow them to. You keep everybody at arm's length; every relationship is on your terms and your terms only. You don't give, you just take. I was a fool to get involved with you in the first place.'

'Then why did you get involved with me?' he asked, turning around once more.

She let out a tiny, almost inaudible, sigh. 'I…I just couldn't help myself…'

Jake straightened to his full height, his eyes clear and focused as they held hers. 'I mean it, Ashleigh, when I say I wasn't involved in any way with Sigrid Flannigan.'

'Why should I believe you?'

'You don't have to believe me, but I would like you to hear my side of it before you jump to any more conclusions.'

'I asked you four and a half years ago and you refused to tell me a thing,' she pointed out stringently.

'I know.' He examined his hands for a moment before reconnecting with her gaze, a small sigh escaping the tight line of his lips. 'Sigrid is a distant cousin of mine. She was conducting some sort of family tree research. To put it bluntly, I wasn't interested. However, she was concerned about some health issues within the family line and I finally agreed to meet her. We met in Paris. She was there on some sort of work-related assignment and, as I was close by, I decided to get the meeting over and done with.'

'And?'

'And I hated every single minute of it.' He dragged his hand through his hair once more. 'She kept going on about how important family ties were and even though we were distantly related we should keep in touch. Apparently I have the questionable honour of being the one and only offspring of Harold Percival Chase Marriott, the last of the male line on that side of the family.' He sent her an accusing look and added, 'Or so I thought.'

'Why didn't you tell me the truth about her?' she asked, choosing to ignore his jibe. 'Why let me believe the worst?'

'I wasn't ready to talk to anyone about my background,' he said. 'I was tempted to tell you a couple of times but I couldn't help thinking that if I told you the truth of my upbringing it would in some way make the differences between us even more marked. Sigrid was an annoying reminder of where I'd come from and I wanted to forget it as soon as I could.'

'So you deliberately let me think she was your lover, even though in doing so it broke my heart?'

He gave an indolent shrug of one shoulder. 'I didn't tell

you what to believe. You believed it without the slightest input from me.'

She let out a choked gasp of outrage. 'How can you say that? You deliberately misled me! You were so cagey and obstructive. You wouldn't even look me in the eye for days on end, much less speak to me!'

'I was angry, for God's sake!' he threw back. 'I was sick to my back teeth with all your tales of how wonderful your family was and how much you missed them. I was sick and tired of being the dysfunctional jerk whose only memories were of being bashed senseless until I could barely stand upright. Do you think I wanted to hear how your mother and father tucked you into your god-dammed bed every night to read you a happy-ever-after story and tell you how much they loved you?'

Ashleigh had no answer.

She felt the full force of his embittered words like barbs in her most tender unprotected flesh. She had no personal hook to hang his experience on. She had never been shouted out; no one had ever raised a hand to her. Her parents had expressed their love for her and her sisters each and every day of their lives without exception. She was totally secure in their devotion. She had absolutely no idea of how Jake would have coped without such consistent assurances of belonging, no idea how he would have coped with nothing but harsh cruelty and the sort of vindictiveness which she suspected had at times known no bounds.

'Is this a good time to interrupt?' Ellie spoke from the doorway, for once her usually confident tone a little dented.

Jake recovered himself first and turned to face her, his expression giving away nothing of his inner turmoil.

'Sure, Ellie.' He stretched his mouth into a small smile. 'Do you need a lift back into town? I'm just about to leave.'

'No,' Ellie insisted. 'I've already promised Lachlan a ride on the bus. He's looking forward to it.'

'So you haven't got your licence yet?' he asked.

Ellie gave him a sheepish grin. 'I've failed the test ten times but I haven't entirely given up hope.'

Jake couldn't help an inward smile. Same old delightful Ellie.

'Is there an instructor left in the whole of Sydney who'll take you on?'

Ellie pretended to be offended. 'I'll have you know I've been with the very best of instructors but not one of them has been able to teach me to drive with any degree of safety.'

'Tell me when you're free and I'll give you a lesson,' he offered. 'After driving in most parts of Europe I can assure you I can drive under any conditions.'

Ellie grinned enthusiastically. 'It's a date. But don't tell me I didn't warn you. Ashleigh will vouch for me. She gave up on lesson two when I ploughed into the back of a taxi.'

Jake swung his gaze to Ashleigh. 'What did she do, rattle your nerves?'

No more than you do, Ashleigh felt like responding. No, she would much rather have Ellie trying to drive in the peak hour any day than face the sort of anger she could see reflected in his dark eyes.

'I have learnt over time to recognise when I am well and truly beaten,' she said instead. 'Ellie needs a much more experienced hand than mine.'

'I don't know…' He rubbed his jaw for a moment in a gesture of wry speculation. 'Seems to me you're pretty experienced at most things.'

Ellie interrupted with a subtle clearing of her throat, Lachlan standing silently by her side, his small hand in hers.

'Excuse me, but we really need to get going if we're going to make the next bus.'

'Are you sure you don't want a lift?' Jake asked again, his glance flicking to the small quiet child at her side.

Before Ellie could answer, Lachlan piped up determinedly, 'I want to go on the bus.'

Jake met the dark eyes of his son, the sombre depths staring back at him sending a wave of something indefinable right through him.

He knew a paternity test was going to be a complete waste of time. This was his flesh and blood and there was clearly no doubt about it. Even the way the boy's hair grew upon his head mimicked his. It was a wonder he hadn't recognised it from the first moment but his shock in discovering Ashleigh had a child had momentarily distracted him. He had still been getting used to the idea of her carrying someone else's progeny when Ellie had dropped her bombshell.

'Don't hurry home.' Ellie filled the small silence. 'You two must have lots to catch up on. I can mind Lachlan tonight. I'm not going out.'

'That won't be necess—'

'That's very kind of you, Ellie.' Jake cut across Ashleigh's rebuttal. 'Your sister and I do indeed have a lot of catching up to do.'

Ellie sent Ashleigh an overly bright smile. 'Well, then... Come on, Lachlan, let's go and get that bus. We'll leave Mummy and Daddy to have a chat all by themselves.'

'Daddy?' Lachlan stopped in his tracks, his expression confused as he looked between his mother and aunt and back again.

Ashleigh sent her sister a now-see-what-you've-done look before bending down to her son.

'Lachlan...'

'Is he my daddy?' Lachlan asked in a whisper, his glance going briefly to the tall silent figure standing beside his mother.

Ashleigh swallowed the lump of anguish in her throat. 'Yes... Jake is your daddy.'

Lachlan's smooth little brow furrowed in confusion. 'But you told me he didn't want to ever know about me.'

'I know…but that was before and now…' She couldn't finish the sentence as her emotions took over. She bit her lip and straightened, turning away to try to pull herself together.

'Lachlan…' Jake stepped into the breach with an out-stretched hand. 'I am very pleased to meet you.'

Lachlan slipped his hand out and touched Jake's briefly, his eyes wide with wonder. 'Are you going to live with Mummy and me now?' he asked.

Jake wasn't sure how to answer. He had never really spoken to a child this young before. How did one go about explaining such complicated relationship dynamics to one so young?

'No,' Ashleigh put in before he could speak. 'Remember I told you? As soon as you go to big school we are going to live with Howard and Mrs Caule.'

Lachlan's shoulders visibly slumped and his bottom lip began to protrude in a pout. 'But I don't like Mrs Caule. She scares me.'

'Lachlan!' she reprimanded him sternly. 'She will be like a pretend granny for you, so don't let me ever hear you speak like that again.'

Ellie tactfully tugged Lachlan towards the door, 'Time to leave, mate.'

Ashleigh opened her mouth to call them both back but caught Jake's warning glance. She let out her breath in a whoosh of frustration and flopped into the nearest seat, dropping her head into her hands.

Jake waited until he heard the front door close on Ellie and Lachlan's exit before he spoke.

'You cannot possibly marry Howard Caule.'

She lifted her head from her hands to stare up at him. *'Excuse me?'*

He met her diamond-sharp gaze with steely determination. 'I won't allow it.'

She sprang to her feet, her hands in fists by her sides.

'What do you mean, you won't allow it?' She threw him a blistering look. 'How the hell are you going to stop me?'

The line of his mouth was intractable as his eyes held hers.

'You cannot possibly marry Howard Caule because you are going to marry me instead,' he said. 'And I will not take no for an answer.'

CHAPTER NINE

ASHLEIGH stared at him for several chugging heartbeats.

'I'm asking you to marry me, Ashleigh,' Jake said into the tight silence.

'*Asking me?*' she shot back once she found her voice. 'No, you're not. You're demanding something you have no right to demand!'

'Don't speak to me of rights,' he bit out. 'I had a right to know I'd fathered a child and you kept that information from me. This is payback time, Ashleigh. You either marry me or face the consequences.'

What consequences? she thought with a sickening feeling in the pit of her stomach. Exactly what sort of consequences was he thinking of?

Jake was a rich man.

A *very* rich man.

How could she even begin to fight someone with his sort of financial influence? The best lawyers would be engaged and before she knew it she would be facing custodial arrangements that would jeopardise her peace of mind for the rest of her life. How would she cope with seeing Jake every second weekend when he came to collect his son on visitation access? How indeed would she cope if he were to gain full custody of Lachlan?

'How long do you think such a marriage would last?' she asked, hoping her panic wasn't too visible, even though her insides were turning to liquid.

'It will last for as long as it needs to last,' he said. 'Every child needs security and, from what little I've seen so far, that little kid is insecure and in need of a strong father figure.'

He'd seen all that in one meeting? His perspicuity amazed her but she didn't let on.

'He's not yet four years old,' she said. 'I would have thought it was a little early to have him written off as an anxious neurotic.'

He gave her a hardened look. 'What did you tell him about me?'

She faced him squarely. 'I told him the truth. I told him his father had never wanted to be a father.'

Jake opened his mouth to berate her but snapped it shut when he saw the defiant glitter in her eyes. He turned away, his stomach clenching painfully as he mentally replayed every conversation he'd had with her in the past on the subject.

No wonder she hadn't told him of the pregnancy.

She was right.

He would have very likely packed her off to the nearest abortion clinic, railroading her into a procedure he had never until this moment given the depth of thought it demanded. Seeing Lachlan this afternoon had made him realise that a foetus was not just a bunch of cells. It had the potential to become a real and living person.

Lachlan was a real and living person.

And he was *his* son.

'I can't change the past, Ashleigh,' he said after another lengthy silence. 'I never wanted this sort of situation to occur but it has occurred and I realise now you probably had little choice in the matter.' He took a steadying breath and continued. 'Given the sort of background you've had, I can see how you would be the very last person to rush off to have a pregnancy terminated. And, as you said earlier, given Ellie's situation, I guess adoption wasn't an option you would have embraced with any sense of enthusiasm.'

Ashleigh witnessed the play of tortured emotions on his face as he spoke and wished she could reach for him and somehow comfort him. They shared the bond of a living and breathing child and yet it seemed as if a chasm the width of the world divided them.

He was devastated by the knowledge of his son's existence; it was his biggest nightmare come true in stark, inescapable reality. It didn't matter how sweet Lachlan was or how endearing his personality, for in Jake's mind there was no escaping the fact that, along with his genetic input, Harold Marriott's blood also flowed through his son's veins.

'I'm sorry, Jake...' she said. 'I don't know what else to say.'

'You can say yes,' he said. 'You can agree to marry me and then this situation will be resolved.'

'How can it be resolved?' she asked. 'How can we pretend things are any way near normal between us?'

'I would hazard a guess that things between us will be very normal. Once we're married we will resume our previous relationship.'

She gaped at him in shock. 'You mean a physical relationship?'

'But of course,' he answered evenly.

'Aren't you forgetting the little but no less significant detail that I already have a fiancé?'

He gave her a cynical look. 'I don't consider Howard Caule your fiancé. He hasn't even convinced you to wear his ring and I can tell by that hungry look in your eyes that he hasn't yet convinced you to share his bed.'

'There are still some men in the world who have some measure of self-control,' she put in with a pointed glare his way. 'Howard has faith. I respect that, even though I don't necessarily share it.'

'Faith?' He let out a scathing snort. 'He would need more than faith to live with you. You are the devil's own temptation from the tip of your head to your toes. I've wanted to throw you onto the nearest flat surface from the first moment I walked into the bar and saw you sitting there twirling your straw in that glass with your fingers.'

His words shocked her into silence. She could feel her skin lifting in physical awareness, tiny goose-bumps breaking out all over her and the pulse of her blood stepping up a pace as her breathing rate accelerated.

'I am engaged.' She finally found her voice but she knew it sounded even less convincing than previously. She looked down at her ringless fingers and repeated, as if to remind herself, 'I am engaged to be married to Howard.'

Jake plucked his mobile phone from his waistband and held it out to her. 'Tell him it's off. Tell him you're marrying me instead.'

Ashleigh stared at the phone as if it were a deadly weapon set to go off at the merest touch.

'I can't do that!'

'Do it, Ashleigh,' he commanded. 'Or I'll do it for you.'

'You can't make me break off my engagement!'

'You don't think so?' he asked, his lip curling sardonically. 'How about if I call dear old Howard and tell him the deal is off?'

Her throat moved up and down in a convulsive swallow.

'There are any number of antique dealers who would gladly snatch up this little load,' he continued when she didn't speak, sending his free hand in an arc to encompass the priceless goods in the room.

'You think you can persuade Howard to release me with such a bribe?' she asked.

'Why don't you call him and find out?' he suggested and pushed the phone towards her again.

She took the phone, her fingers numbly pressing in the numbers.

'Howard?'

'Ashleigh!' Howard's tone was full of delight. 'How was your day?' He hardly paused for her to respond before he went on. 'Do you remember that consignment from Leura that I'd thought we'd lost to the opposition? Well, you'll be thrilled to know that the family of the deceased have decided to give us the deal after all. Isn't that wonderful news? With the consignment you're getting from Jake Marriott we'll be the toast of the town come the antiques fair!'

'Howard...Jake has met Lachlan.'

'My mother, of course, is beside herself,' Howard rambled on excitedly. 'She and my father never imagined the heights I would aspire to, but I have you to thank for that, for without your—'

'Howard—' she interrupted him '—Jake knows about Lachlan.'

'I know it is early days but it will be in all the papers. Howard Caule Antiques will be the premier...' Howard took a small breath. 'What did you say?'

Ashleigh's eyes avoided Jake's as she said into the phone, 'Jake knows Lachlan is his son.' She took an unsteady breath and continued, 'He has asked me to marry him.'

There was a tiny beat of silence before Howard asked, 'What answer did you give him?'

'How do you think I answered?'

Howard let out a long sigh. 'Ashleigh, I know you've done your very best to hide it from me, but I've known for a long time now that you don't really love me.'

'But I—'

'It's all right, Ashleigh—' he cut through her protest '—I understand, I really do. You still have feelings for—'

'Is this about the consignment?' she asked sharply.

'How could you think that of me, Ashleigh?' The hurt in his tone was unmistakable. 'I would gladly let them go to someone else if I thought by insisting you marry me instead of Jake you would be happy. You are never going to be happy until you sort out your past with Jake and we both know it.'

Ashleigh clutched the phone in her hand with rigid fingers, annoyed that Jake was quite clearly hearing every word of her fiancé's.

'You'll have to go through with it,' Howard insisted. 'If not for Lachlan's sake, then for mine.'

'What do you mean?' she asked, her heart plummeting in alarm.

'Jake has a prior claim. He's the child's father, after all. I could never stand in his way; it wouldn't be right. It wouldn't be decent. It wouldn't be moral.'

'But what about us?' she asked in an undertone, turning her back on Jake's cynical sneer.

'Ashleigh.' Howard's voice was steady with resignation. 'You know how much I care for you, but I've known for a long time you don't really feel the same way about me. My mother has been concerned about it for ages. We could have been married months ago, but you wouldn't commit. Doesn't that tell you something?'

She found it difficult to answer him. She *had* been stalling, almost dreading the day when her life would be legally tied to his, in spite of her very real gratitude for all he'd done for her both professionally and personally.

Ashleigh chanced a glance in Jake's direction and noted the self-satisfied curl of his lip with a sinking feeling in her belly.

She turned her back determinedly and spoke to Howard once more. 'I'm sorry about this, Howard…I didn't mean to hurt you like this. You've been so good to me and Lachlan.'

'Don't worry,' Howard said. 'We will always be friends. Anyway, it's not as if we won't see each other. You do still work for me, remember?'

'Yes…'

Jake reached across and took the phone out of her hand and spoke to Howard. 'Caule, Jake Marriott here. Ashleigh won't be working for you once this consignment is delivered to your showroom. I have other plans for her.'

'Oh…I see… Well, then, I wish you all the best, both of you, and Lachlan, too, of course…' Howard's words trailed off.

'We should have this deal stitched up in the next week. It's been good doing business with you, Caule,' Jake said.

'Yes, yes, of course…marvellous to do business with you, Mr Marriott. Absolutely marvellous. Goodbye.'

'What a prick,' Jake muttered as he clipped the phone back on his belt.

Ashleigh stood stiff with rage, her eyes flashing with sparks of fury.

'You arrogant jerk!' She pushed at his chest with one hand. 'How dare you take over my life? "I have other plans for her" indeed! Who the hell do you think you are?'

Jake captured her hand and held it against the wall of his chest.

'I am your son's father and as soon as I can arrange it I will be your husband.'

'You can't cancel my job just like that!'

'I just did.'

'Exactly what plans have you in store for me?' she sniped. 'Licking your boots every day?'

He gave her mouth a sizzling glance before raising his eyes back to her flashing ones.

'No. I was thinking of you going a little higher than that.'

She was incensed by his blatant sexual invitation, her cheeks flaming as a flood of intimate memories charged through her brain.

'I don't want to marry you! I hate you!'

His hand tightened as she tried to remove herself from his hold.

'You don't hate me, Ashleigh,' he said, tugging her even closer, the hard wall of his body shocking her into silence. 'You want me. That's why you've been constructing all those silly little barriers of no touching and no looking and so on because you are so seriously tempted to fall into bed with me. You know you are. It's always been the same between us. From the very first day we met in London, the chemistry between us took over. Neither of us had any chance of holding it back.'

'Your ego is morbidly obese!' she threw at him. 'I have no desire to fall into bed with you.'

'Do you think if you say that enough times you will eventually convince yourself?' he asked. 'Don't be a fool, Ashleigh. I can feel your desire for me right here and now; it's like a pulse in your blood, the same pulse that is beating in mine.' He pressed the flat of her palm over his heart. 'Can't you feel it?'

Ashleigh's eyes widened as his drumming heartbeat kicked against her palm, her mouth going dry as his coal-black eyes glinted down at her with undisguised desire.

She could feel his strong thighs against hers, her soft stomach flattened by the flat hard plane of his, the heat and throb of his growing arousal reaching towards her tantalisingly, temptingly and irresistibly.

Her eyes flickered to his mouth and her breath tripped in her throat as his head came down. She felt the brush of his breath over her mouth just before he touched down, the gentle pressure of his mouth on hers so unlike the hectic passion-driven kisses of the past. For some reason it made it all the more difficult for her to move away. It felt so wonderful to have her lips tingle and buzz with sensation as his caressed hers in a series of barely there kisses.

She felt the intimate coiling of their mingled breaths inside her mouth as he deepened the kiss, the sexy rasp of his tongue sliding along hers, rendering her legs useless.

Her tongue retreated and then flickered tentatively against his, a hot spurt of arrant desire shooting upwards from between her thighs, making her stomach instantly hollow out. She felt the smooth silk of desire anointing her inside as his hardened erection burned into her belly with insistent pressure. Her body remembered how he filled her so completely, privately preparing itself for the intimate onslaught of his passion-driven body surging into her with relentless clawing need.

Her thoughts and memories were in the end betraying her. She had been so determined to push him away. She had wanted to clutch at whatever rag of pride she could to cover herself but it was hopeless. He was right; the chemistry they felt was far too strong to ignore. The air almost crackled with it every time they were in the same room, let alone in each other's arms as they were now.

Jake scooped her up just as she thought her legs were going to fail, and carried her through to his childhood bedroom, coming down hard on the mattress with her, his weight on her a heavy but delicious burden.

He fed off her mouth like a man who had been starved for too long, his lips greedy, ravenous and relentless. Ashleigh kissed him back with the same grasping desperate hunger, her lips swelling beneath the pressure of his, her hands already tearing at his clothes. She tugged his T-shirt out of his jeans and he shrugged himself out of it and sent it hurling across the room, drawing in a ragged gasp as she went for the waist-band of his jeans.

Her eyes drank in the sight of him, the fully engorged length of him, as she pulled away the covering of his tight-fitting underwear. His sharp groan of pleasure as her fingers ran over him lightly sent another burst of liquid need between her legs.

He pushed her hand away and lifted her top, pushing her bra off her straining breasts without even stopping to unfasten it properly. She sucked in a scalding little breath as his mouth closed around one tight aching nipple, the sensation of his teeth scraping her making her hover for a moment in that sensual sphere located somewhere between intense pleasure and exquisite pain.

He left her breasts for a moment while he shucked himself out of his jeans, his shoes thudding to the floor, coming back over her with determined hands to deal with the rest of her clothes. She heard the sound of a seam tearing but was way beyond caring. His hands were on her naked flesh, hot and heavy, rough almost, unleashing yet another trickle of sensual delight right through her.

Feeling his naked skin on hers from chest to thigh was almost too much sensation for her to deal with at once. Her brain was splintering with the electrifying pulse of his body on hers, the probing, searching thickened length of him between her legs.

Suddenly he was there, the force of his entry arching her back as she welcomed him without restraint, her body so ready for him she had trouble keeping her head. She wanted to linger over the feel of him, draw in the scent of their combined arousal to store away for private reflection, but his pace was too hard and fast and she got carried along with the tidal wave of it. She felt the tightening of her intimate muscles, the swelling of her most sensitised point rising to meet each of his determined thrusts.

As if sensing she was close he backed off, withdrawing slightly, his mouth lightening its pressure on hers.

She dragged her mouth from under his and clutched at his head with both of her hands, her eyes searching his face. 'Don't stop now,' she begged in a harsh whisper. 'You can't possibly stop now!'

His mouth twisted into a rueful grimace and he sank into her warmth again, the tightly bunched muscles of his arms either side of her as he supported his weight indicating the struggle he was undergoing to keep some measure of control. 'I shouldn't even be doing this,' he said, his voice tight with tension. 'I'm not wearing a condom.'

'It's all right,' she gasped as he sank a little deeper, her hands going to his buttocks, digging in to hold him where she most wanted him.

'Are you on the pill?' he asked, stilling for a moment.

The pill? Oh, God, when was the last time she'd taken the pill? What was today…? Friday… Surely she had taken it some time this week? She had become a little careless… It wasn't as if Howard had ever…

'Are you on the pill?' he repeated.

'Yes,' she said, mentally crossing her fingers.

'I'll pull out just in case,' he said.

'No!' She grasped at him again, her eyes wild with need. 'You don't have to do that.'

He gave her a sexy smile. 'There are other ways of dealing with it, don't you remember?'

She did remember.

That was the whole trouble.

She remembered it all; the poignant intimacy of taking him in her mouth to relieve him whenever there hadn't been enough time to linger over the preliminaries.

His eyes burned into hers as he began his slow sensuous movements again, each surge and retreat pulling at her with exquisite bone-melting tenderness.

His mouth came back to hers and she sighed with relief,

her legs gripping him tightly, not giving him another chance to pull away.

She felt each and every deep thrust of his body, even felt him nudge her womb where his son had been implanted with his seed, and a great wave of overwhelming emotion coursed through her.

She loved this man.

He was her world. Her life had started the day she'd met him and the only reason it had continued after they'd broken up was because she had carried a part of him away with her.

They were forever joined by the bond of their child and no matter how much he hated being a father and was only offering to marry her out of a sense of duty, she still loved him and knew she would do so until the day she drew her very last breath…

Jake gritted his teeth as he tried to hold back his release. He closed his eyes and counted backwards, trying to think of something unpleasant to focus on instead, but it was no good. The pressure building in him was just too strong. He felt like a trigger-happy teenager with Ashleigh, instead of a thirty-three-year-old man who was always in control.

Always.

'Oh, God!' He felt himself tip over, the emission of pleasure sending shockwaves of shivering ecstasy right through him, great deep racking shudders of it, until he collapsed in the circle of Ashleigh's arms.

He waited for five or so heartbeats of silence.

'I'm sorry.' He eased himself up on his arms to look down at her. 'That was so selfish and crass of me.'

Ashleigh reached up and touched the line of his lean jaw where a tinge of red was already pooling.

'No…don't apologise.'

'I couldn't hold back,' he said, his breathing still a little choppy. 'You have this weird effect on me. I feel about sixteen when I'm near you. All out-of-control hormones, no finesse, no foreplay, just full-on selfish lust.'

'You're not selfish…' She traced her fingertip over the line of his top lip lingeringly.

He took her finger into his mouth and sucked on it, hard.

Her eyes glazed over with unrelieved need and he released her finger, pressing her hand back to the mattress beside her head.

She knew what that look in his eyes meant and her stomach folded over as he moved down her body.

'You don't have to…*oh!*'

He lifted his head for a moment and sent her a spine-loosening look. 'I do have to, baby. I owe you.'

'I…I…' She gave up when his tongue separated her, hot bursts of pleasure sending every thought out of her brain.

She was mindless under his touch, a touch her body remembered like a secret code. Her senses leapt in acute awareness, her pleasure centre tightening to snapping point, each sensitive nerve stretched beyond endurance until it was beyond her capacity to contain it. She felt the rising waves go over her head, crashing all around her, fragmenting her consciousness until she was a mindless, limbless melting pool of nothingness…

Ashleigh wasn't sure how long the silence continued.

She lay with her eyes closed, not sure she was quite ready to meet Jake's penetrating gaze. She knew she had let herself down terribly. Falling into his arms like a desperado was hardly going to give her the ground she needed to maintain her pride.

What a mess!

She gave a painful inward grimace. The irony of it all was gut-wrenching to say the very least. Four and a half years ago all she had wanted was a marriage proposal from him, a promise of security and a future family they could nurture together in the same wonderful way her parents had done for her sisters and her. Instead, she had left him, pregnant, terrified and alone, knowing she had no future with him while she carried his child.

Had he ever cared for her?

He had never said the words. Those three simple words that had been uttered every day of her life in her family: I love you.

No. Jake had never said he loved her. He told her he desired her, he had overwhelmed her with the physical demonstration of his need for her, but he had not once said he loved her.

She felt the shift of the mattress as he got off the narrow bed and opened her eyes, not all that surprised to encounter the stiff line of his back turned towards her as he reached for his clothes.

'How long do you think it will take to get this place clear of all of this stuff?' he asked, zipping up his jeans and turning to face her.

Ashleigh had to fight not to cover herself. Some remnant of pride insisted she pretend she was totally unaffected by what had just transpired. She crossed her ankles and, releasing her hair from behind her neck, met his dark, unreadable eyes.

'I can get the house cleared within a few days,' she said. 'I haven't finished assessing it all, but that can be finalised in Howard's showroom.'

'Good,' he said, reaching for his discarded T-shirt. 'I want to get started on renovating so we can move in as soon as we are married.'

She took immediate offence at his assumption that she was simply going to fall in with his plans. 'Aren't you assuming a little too much?' she asked. 'I don't remember agreeing to marry you.'

His scooped up her clothes from the floor and tossed them towards her, his eyes sending her a warning. 'Get dressed. I want to meet with your family tonight to discuss the wedding arrangements.'

She flung herself off the bed and threw her clothes to one side, beyond caring that she was totally naked.

'You can take a running jump, Jake Marriott,' she snapped at him furiously. 'Do you think my parents are going to go along with your plans? I think I know them a little better than you do.' She folded her arms across her heaving breasts and added bitterly, 'Besides, I can't see my father giving his permission.'

'You're twenty-four years old, Ashleigh,' he pointed out neatly, his eyes flicking briefly to the upthrust of her breasts. 'I hardly think we need to have anyone's permission to get married.'

'I can't believe you want to go through with this. You've always been so against the institution of marriage. The fact that we share a child doesn't mean we have to get married.'

'No, but I have decided that I want to marry you and marry you I will.'

She sent him a caustic glare. 'Well, for one thing, your proposal certainly needs a little polish.'

'Yeah, well, I've never done it before so I'm sorry if it's a bit rough around the edges,' he said with an element of gruffness.

She turned away to step into her clothes, her fingers totally uncooperative under his silent watchful gaze. She bit back a curse as the zip on her skirt nicked the bare skin of her hip, the sudden smarting of tears in her eyes frustrating her. Why couldn't she be more in control around him? Why did he always reduce her to such a quivering emotional wreck?

She turned around at last, determined to have the last word, but he'd already gone. She stared at the wood panel of the door for endless moments, the scent of their recent lovemaking lingering in the air until she felt as if she was breathing the essence of him into her very soul…

CHAPTER TEN

ASHLEIGH drove away from Jake's house with a scowl of resentment distorting her features, her emotions in such disarray she could barely think.

She knew it was unreasonable of her, but a part of her felt intensely annoyed that Howard hadn't fought for her. She knew it was because of the sort of person he was, principled and self-sacrificing, the very qualities she'd been drawn to in her desperate quest for security. But he had caved in to Jake's demands without a single whimper of protest. And it totally infuriated her that Jake had borne witness to it; every time she recalled that self-satisfied smirk on his face her rage went up another notch.

She was far too angry to go home to face her family. She knew Ellie would hold on her promise to mind Lachlan for the evening, so instead of taking the turn to her parents' house, she drove on until she came to Balmoral Beach, a sheltered bay where she'd spent most of her childhood playing in the rock pools and swimming in the jetty enclosure.

She kicked off her shoes and walked along the sand until she came to Wyargine Reserve at the end of the beach, standing at the edge and looking out to sea, the evening breeze ruffling her hair.

After a while the breeze kicked up a pace and her bare

arms started to feel the slight nip in the evening air. She turned and went back the way she'd come, stepping over the rocky ground with care, her shoes still swinging from her hand.

Walking back along the Esplanade, she saw a slim figure jogging towards her and stopped as she recognised her sister Mia.

'Hey there, Ashleigh,' Mia chirped without a single puff. 'I thought you'd be home preparing for the celebrations tonight.'

Ashleigh frowned. 'Celebrations…celebrations for what?'

Mia gave her a rolling-eyed look. 'Your marriage, of course! Jake is around there now. He's brought French champagne. Loads of it. Mum and Dad are thrilled to bits.' She jogged up and down on the spot and continued. 'It was *so* romantic. Jake asked for a private meeting with Dad. How sweet is that? No one but no one asks a woman's father for her hand in marriage any more. Dad was really impressed. Mum was howling like an idiot, of course, and Lachlan has his chest out a mile wide.'

Ashleigh just stared at her, unable to think of a single thing to say. Her family had fallen in with Jake's plans without even consulting her to see if it was what she wanted.

'Is something wrong, Ash?' Mia stopped bouncing from foot to foot to peer at her. 'You do want to marry him, don't you? I mean Howard was all right, but he doesn't exactly ooze with sensuality the way Jake does.' She gave a chuckle of amusement, her grey-blue eyes sparkling cheekily. 'I could never quite imagine Howard dropping his trousers and going for it up against the kitchen bench. In fact, I can't imagine him doing it at all.'

'You are so incredibly shallow sometimes,' Ashleigh bit out and began to stalk back to her car.

'Hey!' Mia grabbed her arm and swung her around to face her. 'What's going on, Ash? Jake wants to marry you. *Hello?*'

She snapped her fingers in front of her older sister's face. 'Isn't that what you've always wanted, to be married to Jake and have a family?'

'He doesn't love me, Mia,' she said bitterly. 'He's only doing it because he found out about Lachlan.'

'I heard about Ellie's little clanger,' Mia said with an expressive little grimace. 'But, all things considered, he's taken it extremely well, don't you think? I mean, a lot of men would refuse to ever speak to you again and try and wriggle their way out of maintenance payments, not to mention insisting on a paternity test.'

'He did insist on one.'

'Oh…' Mia looked a little taken aback. 'Well…I guess that's understandable. I mean, you haven't seen him for years; Lachlan could easily have been someone else's kid.'

Ashleigh sent her a quelling look.

'I mean if you were any other sort of girl…which, of course, you're not,' Mia amended hastily.

They fell into step as they continued along the Esplanade and Mia tucked her arm through her sister's affectionately. 'You know something, Ashleigh, this is like a dream come true. Lachlan now has a father—his real father. I can already see how happy it has made him. Sure he's a little shy around Jake, but he keeps looking up at him with this big wide-eyed look of wonder and it just makes my heart go all mushy.'

Ashleigh kept walking, not trusting herself to respond.

'Jake even brought him a present,' Mia continued. 'It's one of those digging trucks. He said he could help him in the garden at Lindfield.'

He had it all planned, Ashleigh thought bitterly. She wasn't being considered in any part of this; even her family had succumbed to his plan to take over her life as if she had no mind of her own.

'Why are you frowning like that?' Mia asked. 'You love him, don't you, Ashleigh? You've always loved him.'

There didn't seem any reason to deny it.

'Yes, but that's not the point,' Ashleigh said, searching for her keys.

'Then what is the point?' Mia asked as they came to a halt beside Ashleigh's car.

Ashleigh shifted her gaze out to sea once more, a small sigh escaping before she could stop it. 'I have always loved Jake. From the moment I met him I felt as if there could never be anyone else who could make me feel that way. When we parted and I came back to Australia, I sort of drifted into a relationship with Howard, more out of a need for security than anything else. I thought if I settled down with some nice decent man I would eventually forget all about Jake.'

'Jake is not exactly the forgettable type,' Mia remarked wryly.

'Tell me something I don't already know.' Ashleigh gave her a twisted smile.

'Have you slept with him yet?'

Ashleigh felt her face start to burn and turned to unlock her car.

'*Ohmigod!*' Mia crowed delightedly. 'I knew it! You have! Look at your face—you're as red as anything!'

Ashleigh threw her a withering glance. 'One day, Mia, I swear to God I'm going to strangle you.'

Mia just laughed. 'I'll see you at home,' she said with her usual grin. 'I just want to run to the point and back again. Unlike you, my heart rate hasn't gone through the roof today.'

Ashleigh got into the car without another word.

Ashleigh had barely got in the door when Lachlan rushed towards her, his little face beaming.

'Look what Daddy gave me!' He held up the shiny truck for her to see.

She gave him an overly bright smile and bent down to kiss the top of his raven-dark head. 'I hope you said a big thank you,' she said.

'He did,' Jake said, stepping out into the hall from the lounge, his eyes instantly meshing with hers.

'I…I need to have a shower…' she said, making her way past him.

'Wait.' His hand fastened on her arm, halting her.

He turned to his son, who was watching them both with large eyes. 'Lachlan, give me five minutes with Mummy and I'll be up to read that story to you I promised earlier.'

Lachlan's face threatened to split into two with his smile. 'You mean just like a real daddy does?' he asked.

'You betcha.'

'And will you tuck me in and get me to blow the light out?'

Jake turned a quizzical glance Ashleigh's way.

'It's a little thing we do,' she answered softly so Lachlan couldn't hear. 'I put my hand on the light switch and as soon as he puffs a breath out I turn it off. It makes him think he's blown it out like a candle.'

'Cute.'

Jake turned back to the hovering child. 'Better get your lungs into gear, mate. That light might prove a bit difficult unless you start practising right now.'

Lachlan scampered off, the bounce in his step stirring Ashleigh deeply.

'He's a nice little kid,' Jake said into the sudden silence.

She raised her eyes to his, catching her bottom lip for a moment with her teeth.

'You left without saying goodbye,' he said. 'I was worried about you. Where have you been?'

'I needed some time alone. I went for walk on the beach.'

'I've told your family of our plans.'

'*Our* plans?' She sent him an arctic look. 'Don't you mean

your plans, meticulously engineered so that I have no way of extricating myself?'

'You know, Ashleigh, I don't quite see what all this fuss you're making is about. You were desperate for marriage all those years ago and now I'm offering it you want to throw it back in my face. What is it with you?'

'You're not marrying me for the right reasons.'

'What do you expect me to do?' he threw back. 'I come back to Australia to tie up my father's estate and suddenly find I have a nearly four-year-old son to a woman who is hell-bent on marrying a man she doesn't even feel a gram of attraction for.'

She blew out a breath of outrage, her hands fisting by her sides as she glared at him. 'What gives you the right to make those sorts of observations? You know nothing of my feelings for Howard.'

'Are you telling me you're in love with Howard Caule?'

'What difference would it make if I told you yes or no? You're still going to force me to marry you.'

'If he was truly in love with you he wouldn't have exchanged you for a houseful of useless antiques,' he said.

'He did not exchange me for the stupid consignment! He cares about me so, unlike you, he put his personal feelings aside so I could be free. It's called self-sacrifice, in case you aren't familiar with the term.'

Jake gave another one of his snorts of cynicism. 'It's called being a prick. If he was man enough he would have been round here by now knocking my teeth out.'

'But then Howard is not a violent man with no self-control,' she said with a pointed look.

She saw the flare of anger in his dark eyes and the sudden stiffening of his body.

'I have never laid a rough hand on you and you damn well know it,' he ground out.

'Yet,' she goaded him recklessly.

His mouth tightened into a harsh line of contempt. 'I see what you're trying to do. You're trying to push me into being the sort of man my father was. But you can't do it, Ashleigh. I am not going to do it. You can goad me all you like, throw whatever names and insults my way you want, but nothing will make me sink to that level. Nothing.'

'Er…' Ellie popped her head around the door, champagne bottle in hand, juggling two glasses in the other. 'Anyone for a drink?'

Jake gave Ashleigh one last blistering look and, excusing himself, informed Ellie he was going upstairs to put his son to bed.

Ashleigh stood rooted to the spot, her legs refusing to move.

'Trouble in paradise?' Ellie came to her, holding out a glass of champagne.

Ashleigh stared at the rising bubbles in the glass she took off her sister and, taking a deep breath, tipped back her head and downed the contents.

'Way to go, Ash!' Ellie grinned. 'God, he's gorgeous when he's angry. How in the world do you resist him?'

How indeed? Ashleigh thought. That was the whole damn trouble. She couldn't resist him. Her pathetic show of last-minute spirit was all an act. She had no intention of refusing to marry him, but her pride insisted she make him think otherwise.

'I'm going to have a shower,' she said, handing her sister her empty glass.

'Will I tell Jake to join you?' Ellie asked impishly.

'You can tell him to go to hell,' she muttered as she pushed past.

'Isn't that where *you've* been all these years?' Ellie said.

Ashleigh didn't answer. She didn't need to. Her baby sister knew her far too well.

* * *

Ashleigh took her time showering, trying to prolong the moment when she would join the rest of the family downstairs, champagne glasses in hand, wide smiles of congratulations on their lips.

She decided against dressing for the occasion and slipped into a pink sundress she'd had for years, not even caring that it was too tight around her bust. She dragged a brush through her still wet hair and, ignoring her make-up kit and perfume, left her room.

She was just about to go in and kiss Lachlan goodnight when she heard the murmur of voices in his room, Lachlan's higher pitched childish insertions once or twice, and the deep burr of Jake's as he finished the story he was reading. She stopped outside the open door, despising herself for eavesdropping but unable to stop herself.

'I love stories about dogs,' Lachlan was saying. 'I've always wanted a puppy but Granny has al…al…'

'Allergies?' Jake offered helpfully.

'Yes, I think that's what it's called. She sneezes all the time and has to have a puffer thing.'

'I had a dog once…a long time ago now,' Jake said. 'Her name was Patch.'

'That's a funny name.' Lachlan chuckled.

'Yeah…I guess…'

'What was she like?'

Ashleigh heard the sound of the mattress squeaking as Jake shifted his weight on the edge of the bed.

'She was the best friend I ever had.'

'Do you still miss her?'

'Sometimes…' Jake sighed and the mattress made another noise as he stood up. 'I should let you get some sleep.'

'Daddy?'

Ashleigh felt her breath lock in her throat and, before she could stop herself, she turned her head so she could see into the room to where Jake was standing looking down at his little son lying in the narrow bed.

'Yes?' Jake asked.

Lachlan's fingers began to fidget with the hem of his racing car sheet, his eyes not quite able to meet his father's.

'Have you changed your mind about wanting to be a daddy?'

It seemed a very long time before Jake answered, Ashleigh thought, her heart thumping heavily as she counted the seconds.

'I've changed my mind about a lot of things, Lachlan,' he said at last. 'Now go to sleep and we'll talk some more tomorrow.'

Jake took a couple of strides towards the door.

'Daddy?'

He turned to look at his son, something inside him shifting almost painfully when he saw the open adoration on the little guy's face.

'I love you, Daddy,' Lachlan said.

Jake swallowed the tight constriction in his throat but, no matter how hard he tried, he just couldn't locate his voice.

'I loved you even when I didn't know who you were,' Lachlan went on. 'You can ask Mummy, 'cause I told her. I've always wanted a daddy.'

Ashleigh hadn't been aware of making a sound but suddenly Lachlan saw her at the door and sent her a big smile.

'Mummy! Can I blow the light out now?' he asked.

'Not until I give you a big kiss goodnight,' she said and, moving past the silent figure of Jake, gathered her son in her arms and squeezed him soundly before kissing the tip of his nose, both his cheeks and each and every one of his little fingertips.

She straightened and went back to the door where the light switch was but as she put her hand out to it Jake's came over the top of hers and held it there.

'On the count of three, Lachlan,' Jake said, his voice sounding even deeper than usual. 'One…two…three!'

The light was extinguished on Lachlan's big puff of breath and he giggled delightedly as he burrowed back into his bedclothes.

Ashleigh slipped her hand out from under Jake's and met his eyes. She'd thought she had seen just about every emotion in those dark depths in the past but never until this moment had she seen the glitter of unshed tears.

'Jake?'

He reached around her to close Lachlan's door softly, his eyes moving away from hers.

'Come on, your parents are waiting to congratulate us,' he said and, without waiting for her, moved down the hall.

Ashleigh watched his tall figure stride away, the set of his broad shoulders so familiar and yet so foreign. She had shared his body that afternoon and yet he did not want to share his heart.

Did he even have one?

Or was it too late?

Had his father destroyed that, along with every other joy he should have experienced as a child?

'Darling!' Gwen Forrester swept her daughter into her arms as soon as she came into the lounge. 'Congratulations! We are so very thrilled for you and Jake.'

Her father came over and hugged her tightly and Ashleigh buried her head into his shoulder, wondering if he knew how confused she really was.

'Jake.' Gwen started bustling about with her usual motherly fuss. 'Come and sit down and have a drink. Mia? Get your brother-in-law-to-be some champagne, or would you prefer a beer?'

'Champagne is fine,' Jake said.

'When are you going to get married?' Ellie asked.

'In a month's time,' Jake answered. 'It takes that long to process the licence.'

'Wow! A month isn't very long,' Mia said. 'Can I be bridesmaid?'

'Me, too!' Ellie put in.

Ashleigh stretched her mouth into a smile but inside she felt her anger simmering just beneath the surface.

'Will you have a big wedding?' Gwen asked.

'No, I don't think—' Ashleigh began but Jake cut her off.

'No point getting married if you don't do it properly.' He sent her a smile. 'After all, Ashleigh has always wanted to be a bride, haven't you, darling?'

She gave him what she hoped looked like a blissful smile although her jaw ached with the effort.

'How did Howard take the news?' Ellie asked, twirling her champagne glass in one hand.

Jake didn't give Ashleigh the chance to respond. His smile encompassed everyone as he said, 'He was a true gentleman. He wanted what was best for Ashleigh and wished us both joy.'

Ashleigh was sure her dentist was going to retire on the work she'd need done after this. She ground her teeth behind her smile and downed the contents of her glass, her head spinning slightly as she set it back down on the nearest surface.

'How soon will you be able to move into the house at Lindfield?' Heath asked.

'It will take most of the month, I'm afraid. I'm starting work on it this weekend,' Jake answered. 'In fact, I was hoping Ashleigh and Lachlan would come with me. It will be our first weekend as a family.'

Ashleigh knew she would look a fool if she said she had other plans so stayed silent.

'Are you sure Lachlan won't be in the way?' Mia gave her sister a mischievous wink.

'I'd like to spend some time with him,' Jake said. 'I won't let him come to any harm. The workmen won't arrive till Monday to do the major renovations, so it will be quite safe.' He turned to Ellie. 'I was hoping to take Ashleigh out tonight to celebrate on our own. Is your offer to babysit still on?'

'Sure!' Ellie beamed. 'Go out and have a good time. In fact, why don't you take her to stay out all night at your hotel? Lachlan won't wake up till morning and it's Saturday tomorrow so there's no rush to get him to crèche or anything.'

'But I—'

'I wouldn't want to impose…' Jake said before Ashleigh could get her protest out.

'Rubbish!' Gwen joined in heartily. 'Go on, the two of you, have some time to yourselves. After all, four and a half years is a lot of time to catch up on.'

'Thank you,' he said and turned to face Ashleigh. 'How long will it take you to get ready, darling?'

How about another four and a half years? she felt like retorting.

'Five minutes,' she said and left the room.

'You're very quiet,' Jake commented once they were on their way to the city a short time later.

She swivelled in her seat to glare at him. 'How could you do that to me?'

'Do what?' He flashed a look of pure innocence her way.

'Act as if you're the devoted fiancé who can't wait to get me all alone.'

'But I can't wait to get you all alone.'

She sucked in a shaky breath as his words hit home, her stomach doing a crazy little somersault.

'That's beside the point…' She floundered for a moment.

'You had no right to pretend everything is perfectly normal, that we've patched things up as if the past didn't happen. Quite frankly I'm surprised my family couldn't see through it.'

'I had a long talk with your father before you came home,' he said. 'I told him I'd changed my mind about marriage and that I wanted to be a real and involved father to Lachlan. I also told him that I would look after you, provide for you and protect you.'

She folded her arms crossly and tossed her head to stare out of the passenger window. 'No doubt you threw in a whole bunch of lies about loving me, too, just for good measure.'

The swish of the tyres on the bitumen was the only sound in the long stretching silence.

Ashleigh silently cursed herself for revealing her vulnerability in such a way. What was she thinking? He hadn't even been able to utter the words to his three-year-old son. What hope did she have of ever hearing them directed at her?

'I saw no reason to lie to your father,' Jake said evenly.

She frowned, trying to decipher his statement, but before she had any success he spoke again.

'Your family want what is best for you, Ashleigh. They know that you haven't been happy for a long time, and to their credit they are prepared to put any past prejudices they may have held against me to one side in order to welcome me into the family.' He sent her a teasing little glance. 'Besides, both your sisters think I'm a much better deal than dear old Howard.'

'I wish you wouldn't speak of him in that way.'

'I still can't believe you were considering marrying him.'

'Yeah? Well, at least he had the decency to ask me,' she threw at him resentfully.

Jake's hands tightened on the wheel as her hard-bitten words hit their mark. He gritted his teeth against the surge of anger he felt. What did she expect? Some promise of blissful happy ever after, when all he could promise was to…*was to what?*

He dragged in a prickly breath and tried to concentrate on the line of traffic ahead, watching as each car edged closer and closer together, as if to nudge the red light signal into changing. His foot hovered on the accelerator, biding his time to go forward, his fingers drumming the steering wheel in increasing agitation.

All he could promise was to what?

CHAPTER ELEVEN

ASHLEIGH was so determined she wasn't going to say another word to Jake for the rest of the journey, if not the rest of the evening, that it took her a quite a while tо realise that he hadn't directed a single word her way for several minutes. She cast him covert glances every now and again as he negotiated the city traffic, but his eyes didn't once turn her way and the stiff line of his mouth clearly indicated that he had no desire to engage in conversation with her.

OK, so he hadn't appreciated her little dig about his forceful proposal.

Fine.

She could handle his stonewalling. It would make for a long and tense evening, but why should she always be the one to smooth things over? Besides, he was the one who'd steamrollered her into committing to a marriage she knew he would never have been insisting on if it wasn't for Lachlan's existence.

How was that supposed to make her feel? He hadn't even tried to pretend to have any feelings for her, other than displaying his usual rampant desire which he no doubt felt for any woman between the ages of nineteen and forty.

Admittedly, he'd somehow convinced her family that things were now all rosy and romantic between them, but she knew that was probably because Howard had always seemed to them to be not quite the right partner for her. Her parents, of course, had known better than to say so out loud, but Mia and Ellie hadn't abided by any such polite boundaries. The open joy on their faces as they'd toasted her engagement to Jake that evening was testament to their relief that she had finally come to her senses. But exactly what was sensible about marrying a man who not only didn't love her but loathed the whole notion of marriage and family life?

The hotel valet parking attendant greeted Jake by name as he drove into the reception bay. Ashleigh stepped out of the car when one of the uniformed bell boys opened her door for her and stood waiting for Jake, who was exchanging pleasantries with another staff member.

'I'll have the young lady's luggage brought up to your room immediately,' the young man said as he took the keys from Jake.

Ashleigh gave an audible snort. Her small tote bag could hardly be described as luggage; she'd barely put a thing in it besides her cosmetics purse and her oldest, most unflattering, nightgown. If Jake thought he was in for a hot night of passion with her in his hotel bedroom he could think again.

'Will you require a reservation for dinner in the restaurant this evening or will you be ordering room service, Mr Marriott?' The concierge asked as they approached reception for Jake to collect his mail.

'Room service will be fine,' Jake answered without even consulting Ashleigh. 'Were there any messages left for me today?'

The concierge handed him two or three envelopes. 'That's all so far. Is there anything else we can do for you, Mr Marriott?'

'Yes.' Jake's mouth tilted into a smug sort of smile. 'Have the bar send up a bottle of your very best champagne and two glasses.'

'Right away, Mr Marriott.' The concierge's eyes went to Ashleigh, standing rigidly to one side. 'May I ask, are we celebrating something special this evening?'

'Yes. Ms Ashleigh Forrester and I are celebrating our engagement and forthcoming marriage,' Jake said and, tucking the envelopes in his back pocket, added, 'Oh… and could you also contact the press and make a formal announcement on my behalf?' He took one of the gold pens off the reception counter and, reaching for a hotel notepad, quickly wrote down what he wanted to appear in the following day's paper and handed it back to the concierge.

'Consider it done, Mr Marriott. And on behalf of the hotel management and staff may I offer you our most sincere congratulations.' He turned towards Ashleigh and gave her a polite smile. 'Nice to meet you, Ms Forrester.'

Ashleigh mumbled something in reply and stumbled after Jake as he led her by the elbow towards the bank of lifts.

Once they were out of earshot of the reception area she tugged herself out of his hold and dusted off her elbow as if to remove something particularly nasty from it before sending him a furious glare. 'You've got a dammed hide!'

Jake pressed the call button without answering and, folding his arms across his chest, leaned indolently against the wall.

Ashleigh felt like stamping her foot in frustration.

'You know what the staff are all thinking, don't you?' she hissed at him. 'They think we're going to hole ourselves up in your room for a night of raunchy sex, fortifying ourselves with champagne and bloody room service!'

Jake's eyes were still and dark as they met her flashing ones. 'Is that a problem for you?'

She let out a whooshing breath. 'Of course it's a problem for me! This time yesterday I was engaged to Howard Caule. What will everyone think when they see tomorrow's paper and hear that you are now my fiancé?'

The lift doors opened and Jake stood back to allow her to enter first. The door hissed shut behind them before he responded smoothly. 'They will think the best man won.'

She let out another infuriated breath. 'This is all a game to you, isn't it, Jake? All this talk about winning and losing, as if I'm some sort of prize that everyone's been bidding for.'

She caught her lip with her teeth and looked away from the glint of satire in his dark eyes. 'I don't want to even be here with you, much less sleep with you,' she said, privately hoping she had the strength of will to follow through on her rash words.

'You know you don't mean that, Ashleigh, so don't go making me get all fired up just so I have to prove it to you.'

She felt a flicker of betraying need between her thighs at his statement, the smouldering fire in his challenging gaze threatening to consume her on the spot.

The lift doors opened and she almost fell out in relief, her lungs dragging in air as if she'd been holding her breath for hours instead of a mere few seconds.

She suddenly felt faint, light-headed and disoriented, the carpeted floor rolling up towards her, the swirling colours getting all mixed up in a stomach-churning pattern that seemed to make the floor unstable beneath her feet…

'Are you all right?'

She heard Jake's voice as if he was speaking to her through a long tunnel, the words rising and falling like an echo, here one second, gone the next.

'I…I think I'm going to… She wobbled, one of her hands clutching at mid-air until she found something strong and immovable to keep her upright.

Jake held her tightly against him as he swiped his key card

to his room and, shouldering open the door, scooped her up and carried her inside, the door clicking shut behind him.

'I…I…I'm going to be sick…' Ashleigh gasped as she put a shaky hand up to her mouth.

'The bathroom is just through—'

Too late.

Ashleigh threw up the contents of her stomach all over his chest.

Jake managed to salvage the cream carpet by tugging his shirt out of his trousers to act as a sort of bib-cum-scoop as he led her to the bathroom. He set her down on the edge of the bath, one hand still holding the contents of his T-shirt as he frowned in concern at the pallor of her face.

'Oh, God…'

She swayed for a moment and then lunged for the toilet bowl. He winced as she threw up again, each harsh tortured expulsion of her throat reminding him of the weeks after she'd left him in London when a daily bottle of Jack Daniels had been his only comfort.

He gingerly removed himself from his T-shirt, leaving it in the bottom of the shower stall, and reaching for one of the hand towels, wet it under the cold tap before applying it to her shockingly pale face.

'Hasn't anyone ever told you never to drink champagne on an empty stomach?' he said, gently mopping her brow.

She gave him a withering glance and looked as if she was about to throw a stinging comment his way when her face suddenly drained of all colour once more and she lurched towards the toilet bowl again.

Jake waited until she was done before handing her the re-rinsed towel again.

Ashleigh buried her face in its cool, refreshing, cleansing folds, wondering if this was some sort of omen for the rest of their future together.

'When was the last time you ate?' Jake asked.

Ashleigh groaned into the towel. '*Please* don't talk about food!'

'How many glasses of champagne did you have at your parents' house?'

'I don't know…two…maybe three…'

'Too many, if you ask me.'

'I didn't ask you.'

'That reminds me,' Jake said, helping her to her feet, his hands on her upper arms gentle but firm. 'It has occurred to me that I haven't actually asked you to marry me.'

Ashleigh stared at him, her stomach still deciding on its next course of action, her throat raw and her eyes and nose streaming.

'You were right to be angry with me,' he continued. 'I didn't ask you, I just told you that we were going to get married. I didn't even give you a choice.'

She opened her mouth and just as rapidly closed it, not sure if words or something a little less socially appropriate was still intent on coming out.

'Ashleigh…' He cleared his throat, his eyes dark and steady on hers. 'Will you marry me?'

Jake stepped backwards as she lunged for the toilet bowl again and flinched as she gave another almighty heave.

She was right after all, he thought wryly as he rinsed out the hand towel yet again.

Maybe he *did* need a little polish on his proposal.

Ashleigh crawled into the shower a few minutes later, way beyond the point of caring that Jake was standing watching her shivering naked under the warm spray. She closed her eyes and let the water run over her, trying to concentrate on staying upright instead of sinking to the floor and disappearing down the drain, which her body seemed to think was a viable option.

'You don't look so good,' Jake said.

She opened one bloodshot eye. 'Thanks…just what a naked woman wants to hear.'

He smiled and reached for a big fluffy white bath sheet, holding it to one side as his other arm brushed past her breast to turn off the shower rose.

Ashleigh stepped into the soft towel he held out and didn't even try and take over the drying of her body herself. Instead she stood like a helpless child as he gently dried her, the softness of the towel and his soothing, caress-like touch making her throat threaten to close over with emotion.

'Do you want me to dry your hair for you?' he asked once he'd wrapped her sarong-wise in a fresh dry towel. 'There's a hairdryer on the wall next to the shaving outlet. I've never done a blow job before but who knows? Like someone else I know, I might prove to have a natural flair.'

She rolled her eyes at him and then wished she hadn't. 'I think I might just lie down for a while…my head hurts.'

He pulled back the bed covers and she climbed in, closing her eyes as soon as her head found the feather-light pillow.

Jake stood watching her for endless moments, wondering if he should have called a doctor or something. But then he remembered what a hopeless head for alcohol she'd had in the past. One drink and she was practically under the table.

His conscience gave him a sharp little prod of recollection which he wanted to push away but couldn't. She had held him off for two dates but on the third he had been so determined to have her that he hadn't thought much beyond getting her clothes off any way he could…

He gave a rough-edged sigh and, before he could stop himself, gently brushed the back of his hand across the velvet softness of her cheek, the feel of her skin under his work-roughened knuckles reminding him of the smooth cream of silk. She mumbled something he couldn't quite catch and, curling up into an even smaller ball, nestled her cheek further into the pillow.

He reached for the bedside chair and sat in it heavily, his head dropping to his hands, his fingers splaying over his forehead.

It was going to be a long night.

Ashleigh woke sometime during the night, her head feeling surprisingly clear but her stomach instantly clamouring for food.

'Did you say something?' Jake's voice came out of the darkness from the other side of the huge bed.

'No…that was my stomach,' she said, her insides giving another noisy rumble.

She felt the slight tilt of the mattress as he reached for the bedside lamp, her pupils shrinking a little when the soft light washed over her.

'What did it say?' he asked, his mouth curving into a small smile.

Don't look below his neck, she warned herself.

'It said it wants some food,' she said, fiddling with the edge of the sheet that only just covered her breasts.

'What sort of food?' Jake got up from the bed and stretched. 'Soup and toast or what about something greasy for a hangover cure?'

'I don't have a hangover,' she said a little tightly.

She sensed rather than saw his smile as he reached for the phone.

'Jake Marriott here, suite fourteen hundred,' he said. 'Can we have some bacon and eggs with a double side of fries?'

Ashleigh threw him a filthy look and he added, 'No, no champagne with that order. We haven't started on the other bottle yet.' He hung up the phone and gave another big stretch, his biceps bulging as he raised his arms above his head, his stomach muscles rippling like rods of steel under a tightly stretched satin sheet.

'Do you have to do that?' she said irritably.

'Do what?' He rolled his shoulders and dropped his arms, his look totally guileless.

She pursed her mouth and edged the sheet a little higher. 'You could at least put something on.'

'You've seen me naked before,' he pointed out. 'Besides, I fell asleep in the chair a little earlier and it made me a little stiff.'

Her eyes went to his pelvis, her cheeks instantly filling with heat. She wrenched her gaze away and fiddled with the sheet to distract herself from his tempting form.

'You know something? You never used to be such a little prude,' he commented. 'I hope Howard hasn't given you a whole lot of hang-ups about sex.'

'I don't have any hang-ups…' She chewed her bottom lip for a moment. 'It's just that…' She paused, not sure it was exactly wise to go on.

'Just what?' he asked.

She raised her eyes to his. 'It's just it's always been such a very physical thing…for you, I mean.'

'And it's not for you?' he asked, holding her gaze.

'Yes, yes, of course it is…but…' She lowered her eyes and began to tug at a loose thread on the sheet, wishing she hadn't drifted into such deep water.

'I don't like the sound of that "but",' he said after a short silence. 'What are you trying to say? That you're still in love with me after all this time?'

She stared at him for five heavy blood-clogging heart-beats.

'Ashleigh?'

There was a discreet tap at the door and their eyes locked for a moment.

'Room service,' a young male voice called out.

Jake reached for his jeans where he'd left them hanging over a chair, stepping into them, zipping them up and running a rough hand through his hair before he moved across to open the door.

Ashleigh hitched the sheet right up to her chin and watched as Jake tipped the young man who carried in the tray of food, waiting until he'd gone again before turning back to her.

'Come on, let's get some food into you, then we can continue that little discussion we were having on sex,' he said.

She propped herself up in the bed with pillows as he carried the tray over. He set it across her lap, giving her a little wink as he snitched a French fry and popped it in his mouth.

She gave him a guilt-stricken look as she suddenly recalled how the evening in his room had started. 'You must have missed dinner…I'm sorry.'

He gave her another one of his wry smiles. 'To be quite frank with you, sweetheart, I didn't feel all that much like food after your little bathroom routine.'

She grimaced and speared a chip with her fork. 'Don't remind me.' She gave a little shudder. '*Yeeuck.* I am never going to drink champagne again. *Ever.*'

He laughed and took another fry. 'You never could handle alcohol. One drink and you are anybody's.'

Her fork froze halfway to her mouth, her eyes slowly meeting his.

His smile faded. 'You know, I didn't actually mean that quite the way it sounded.'

'Yes, you did.' She pushed the food away in disgust.

'No!' He rescued the tilting tray and set it to one side before coming back to untie her hands from where she'd crossed them tightly over her breasts.

'Hey.' He gave her fists a little squeeze. 'I didn't mean to insult you. The truth is, I have never forgotten what it was like that first time…' His throat moved up and down in a swallow. 'I've tried to, believe me, but it just won't go away.'

She tossed her head to one side. 'You've probably had hundreds of lovers since then who have imprinted themselves indelibly on your sexual seismic register.'

'Maybe—' he gave a shrug of one shoulder '—but, as far as I recall, no four point fours.'

Her eyes came back to his, her look indignant. *'Four point four?* Is that all I rated?'

He tapped her on the end of her nose, the edges of his mouth tipping upwards sexily. 'Thought that would get a rise out of you.'

She reached past him for the tray of food and scooped up a rasher of bacon without the help of cutlery and stuffed it in her mouth, her blue eyes flashing sparks of fire as she chewed resolutely.

'You know something, Ashleigh,' he said, spearing a French fry with her abandoned fork. 'You're really something when you're all fired up.'

'Stop pinching my fries.' She slapped his hand away. 'I want them all to myself.'

He laid the fork down and, moving the tray just out of her reach, kissed her hard upon the mouth.

Ashleigh blinked up at him when he lifted his mouth off hers.

'What was that for?' she asked.

He picked up a French fry and held it near her tightly clamped lips. 'Open.'

She opened.

'That's good.' He smiled as she chewed and swallowed. 'Now we're getting somewhere.'

Ashleigh wasn't sure she wanted to know exactly what he meant. Besides, her stomach was still screaming out for food and he seemed perfectly happy to pass it to her, morsel by morsel. All she had to do was chew and swallow and avoid his probing gaze.

She opened her mouth on a forkful of easy-over egg and wickedly fattening bacon and closed her eyes.

Heaven.

CHAPTER TWELVE

ASHLEIGH woke the next morning to find Jake sitting fully dressed in one of the chairs near the bed, his dark gaze trained on her, his expression thoughtful.

'Hi,' he said, a small smile lifting the edges of his mouth.

'Hi.' She eased herself upright, securing the sheet around her naked breasts, wondering what was going on behind those unreadable eyes.

'I've been doing some thinking while you were sleeping,' he said after a little silence.

She gave him a wary look without responding.

He ran a hand through his hair and continued. 'I realised during the night that from the very first day I met you in London I fast-tracked you into a physical relationship. I did it to you again recently.' He held her gaze for a moment or two. 'I want to prove to you that I'm serious about making our marriage work by being patient, a quality you're not used to seeing in me.' He drew in a breath and added, 'In the next four weeks leading up to our wedding I promise not to kiss you, touch you or even look at you in a sexual way when we are alone.' He paused as if waiting for her reaction to his announcement but when she remained silent he shifted his gaze and, getting to his feet, walked over to the window and looked down at the street below, his back turned towards her. 'I want to get to know my son and start to build the sort of family structure I missed out on as a child.'

'I see…'

He turned back to face her, his expression giving nothing away. 'Four weeks isn't all that long when you consider we'll have the rest of our lives together, don't you agree?'

Ashleigh wasn't sure how to answer. She had spent four and a half miserable years missing him and now that he was back, four minutes without him touching her hurt like hell. How would she ever get through it?

'If that's what you want…' Her eyes fell away from the intensity of his.

He eased himself away from the window sill where he'd been leaning and reached for the room service menu. 'Let's have breakfast and get going. I want to spend the day with Lachlan. He's probably wondering where we both are.'

Ashleigh sat on the back step at Jake's house and watched as Lachlan helped his father complete the tree-house they'd been building in the elm tree.

Almost four weeks had passed and Jake had stuck to his promise; not once had he touched her while they were alone.

She gave a twisted little smile.

With all the rush of wedding preparations they'd had precious little time by themselves and she couldn't help wondering if he'd planned it that way to make it easier on himself. As for herself, she had ached for him relentlessly, her body tingling with awareness whenever his dark as night eyes rested on her.

Now, with a day to go before they were officially married, she could barely contain her nervous anticipation. Her legs felt weak and shaky whenever he smiled at her, the slightest brush of his hand against hers stirring her into a frenzy of clawing need.

'What do you think, Ashleigh?' Jake asked as he strode

towards her with Lachlan's small hand tucked in his. 'Do you think it'll do?'

She smiled at the pure joy on Lachlan's grubby face as he gazed up at his father. Her son had blossomed in a matter of days as he'd soaked up the presence of Jake. He had clung to him during every waking hour as if frightened he might suddenly disappear. It had made Ashleigh's heart swell to witness the sheer devotion on his little face and she knew that no matter what happened in her relationship with Jake in the future, Lachlan would always want to be in contact with his father and she would do nothing to come between them.

'It looks wonderful,' she said.

Jake helped her to her feet, his work-roughened palm sending a riot of sensations through her fingers to the centre of her being as his eyes meshed with hers.

'This time tomorrow,' he said on the tail-end of an expelled breath.

She didn't trust herself to answer without betraying herself.

Jake's eyes left hers to look at the house, his small sigh of approval speaking volumes. 'It looks like a real home now, doesn't it?'

Ashleigh followed the line of his gaze. The house had been painted inside and out, the threadbare blinds replaced with the soft drape of curtains and the floors polished, with new rugs laid out here and there for comfort and cosiness. The furniture was all modern and comfortable, all except for one small writing desk that Jake wanted to keep because it had been his mother's. The rest of the antiques had gone along with the outdated appliances in the kitchen; it was now newly appointed and the bathrooms beautifully refurbished as well.

The front and back gardens had been tidied, Jake doing a lot of the physical labour himself with Lachlan faithfully by his side.

'Yes,' she agreed. 'It looks like a real home.'

'Can I play with my cars now, Daddy?' Lachlan asked, tugging on Jake's hand.

'Sure,' Jake said, ruffling his hair. 'Thanks for helping me. I couldn't have done that last bit without you.'

Lachlan's proud grin threatened to split his face in two. 'I love you, Daddy.' He hugged the long legs in front of him. 'I love you *this* much!' He squeezed as hard as he could, the sound of his childish little grunt of exertion making tears spring to Ashleigh's eyes.

She blinked them back as she watched Jake bend down to his son's level, his voice gruff with emotion. 'I love you, too, mate. More than I can say.' His eyes shifted slightly to meet Ashleigh's over the top of their son's dark head. 'Sometimes words are just not enough.'

Lachlan scampered off but Ashleigh hardly noticed. She'd never heard Jake say those three little words to anyone before, not to her certainly, and not even to Lachlan until now, even though Lachlan had said it to him many times over the last four weeks.

She ran her tongue over her dry lips as Jake straightened to his full height, his body so close to hers that she could feel the heat of it against her too sensitive skin.

He gave her a small rueful smile. 'I promised myself a long time ago that I'd never say those words again.'

'Why?' Her voice came out soft as a whisper.

There was a small but intense silence as his eyes held hers.

'Remember I told you about my dog?'

She nodded.

'I really loved that dog,' he said after another little pause. 'But as soon as I said those words to her my father heard me and got rid of her.'

'Oh, Jake…' She bit her lip to stop it from trembling.

He took something out of his pocket and silently handed it to her.

She looked down at the decayed strip of red-coloured leather lying across her hand, the small silver buckle jangling against something metal attached to it. She turned the tiny name tag over to see the name Patch engraved there.

'He didn't send her to the country after all,' Jake said. 'He killed her and buried her in the garden. I found her body, or at least what was left of it, and her collar a few days ago.'

Ashleigh lifted her gaze to his, tears rolling down her cheeks as she saw the raw emotion etched on his face.

'Jake…'

'Shh.' He pressed a finger against her lips to stop her speaking. 'Let me get this out while I still can.' He took a deep breath and let the words tumble out at last. 'I love you. I guess I've wanted to tell you that from the first moment I met you but I was too cowardly to do so. Instead, I hurt you immeasurably, wrecking my own life in the process, robbing myself of the precious early years of my son's life. Can you ever forgive me for the pain I've caused you?'

She was openly blubbering by now but there was absolutely nothing she could do to stop it. 'There's nothing to forgive…I love you…I've loved you for so long…I…I…'

Jake crushed her to him, his face buried in the fragrant cloud of her hair. 'I don't deserve you…I don't deserve Lachlan either. You're both so incredibly beautiful…I feel like I'm going to somehow spoil your life now that I am in it again.'

'No!' Ashleigh grasped at him with both hands, holding his head so his eyes were locked on hers. 'Don't *ever* think that. I have spent four and a half of the unhappiest years of my life without you. I don't think I would survive another day if you were to leave me now. You are the most wonderful person. I know that. I know it in my heart. You are nothing like your father. Look at the way Lachlan loves you; how can you doubt yourself? I certainly don't. I *know* who you are, Jake. You might bear your father's name but you don't have anything else of him inside you. I just know it.'

His dark eyes were bright with moisture as he looked down at her. 'I didn't realise loving someone could be so painful,' he said. 'When I saw you at the bar that night I could barely breathe. I was so determined that I could handle seeing you again but one glimpse of you turned me inside out with longing.'

'Oh, Jake…' She looked up at him with shining eyes. 'What a silly pair of fools we were. I was feeling exactly the same way! I had to stop myself reaching out to touch you to make sure you were really back in my life after all that time. I loved you so much and was so scared you'd see it and make fun of me.'

His eyes grew very dark and his voice husky and deep with emotion. 'Promise me you'll keep telling me you love me, Ashleigh. I'm not sure if my mother ever told me because I was so young when she died, but you're the first person I can remember ever saying those three little words. You have no idea how wonderful they make me feel.'

'I promise.'

He brushed the crystal tears spilling from her eyes with a gentle finger. 'I love you.'

'I know…I can hardly believe it's true…'

'You'd better believe it because I'm going to say it about ten times a day to make up for all the times I should have said it in the past.'

'Only ten times a day?' She gave him a little teasing smile. 'What else are you going to do with your time?'

His eyes glittered as they held hers. 'You know all those kitchen benches that were recently fitted inside?'

She gave a little nod as her stomach flipped over itself in anticipation. 'I did wonder why you wanted such a lot of bench space. Have you suddenly developed an intense passion for cooking?'

He gave her a bone-melting look and brought her even closer. 'I'm not much of a cook but I'm sure between the two of us we'll think of something to do with all that space. Don't you agree?'

Ashleigh just smiled.

EPILOGUE

Eight months later...

ASHLEIGH was in one of her nesting moods again. Ever since she'd found out she was pregnant she'd been fussing about the house, rearranging things to suit her ever changing whims; now with only a month to go she was virtually unstoppable.

Jake smiled fondly as she instructed him to shift yet another piece of furniture, her swollen belly brushing against him as she moved past him.

He still found it hard to believe he was married with a son and a little daughter on the way. His life had changed in so many ways but each one was for the better. His bitterness about the past had gradually faded to a far off place which he rarely visited now. Ashleigh's love had healed him just as surely as his son's devotion, which still brought a clogging lump to his throat every time he looked into those dark eyes that so resembled his own.

'No...I think it looks better back over there,' Ashleigh said, turning around to look at him. 'What do you think, darling?'

His eyes ran over her, lingering for a moment of the full curve of her breasts before meshing with her blue gaze. 'If I told you what I was thinking right now you'd probably blush to the very roots of your hair.'

She smiled one of her cat-that-swallowed-the-canary smiles. 'What exactly are you thinking?'

He gently backed her up against the writing desk, his hand going to her belly, his open palm feeling for the movement of his child. 'That you are the sexiest mother I've ever seen and if it wasn't for Ellie and Mia bringing Lachlan back any minute now I would have my wicked way with you.'

Ashleigh felt her legs weaken and grasped at the writing desk behind her to steady herself. The fragile timber gave a sudden creak and part of the front panelling of the top drawer came away in her hand.

'Oh, no!'

'Did you hurt yourself?' Jake's tone was full of concern as he steadied her.

She shook her head, turning to look at the damage she'd done to his mother's desk.

'No, but—' She stopped as she stared at the small compartment that had been hidden behind the panelling she'd inadvertently removed. In the tiny thin space was an envelope.

She took it out, turning it over in her hands, her eyes briefly scanning the feminine writing and the name written there before she handed it to Jake.

'I think it's a letter of your mother's,' she said. 'It's addressed to someone in New Zealand. She mustn't have been able to post it before she died…'

Jake opened the envelope and read through the pages one by one, his dark eyes absorbing each and every word, the only sound in the room the soft rustle of paper that hadn't seen the light of day in close to thirty years.

'What does it say?' Ashleigh asked softly as she saw the sheen of tears begin to film over his eyes.

Jake drew in a deep breath and looked at her. 'You were right, Ashleigh. You knew it all along.'

'Kn-knew what?' Her voice wobbled along with Jake's chin as she watched him do his best to control his emotion. 'W-what did I know?'

'This is a letter to my father,' he said, wiping a hand across his eyes. 'My *real* father.'

'You mean…?'

'Harold Marriott was infertile.' He looked down at the words he'd just read as if to make sure they hadn't suddenly disappeared. 'He had testicular cancer as a young man and after the treatment was unable to father a child.'

'So you're not…' She couldn't get the words past the sudden lump in her throat.

'My mother was five months pregnant when she married him,' he said. 'She hadn't told my real father of my existence because he was already married, but when she knew she was dying she decided to write to him…but, probably due to her sudden decline in health, the letter was never sent.'

'Oh, Jake…'

Jake pulled her to him and hugged her tightly, his head buried into her neck. 'You were right, Ashleigh. You were right all along. I am *not* my father's son.'

Ashleigh looked up at him, her eyes brimming over. 'I would still love you even if you were his son. I'm happy for you that you're not but it makes absolutely no difference to me. I love you and I always will, no matter what.'

No matter what. Jake breathed the words deep into his soul, where Ashleigh's love had already worked a miracle of its own.

HARLEQUIN *Presents*

We're delighted to announce that

A Mediterranean Marriage

**is taking place in
Harlequin Presents™ —
and you are invited!**

Leon Aristides believes in money, power and
family, so he insists that the woman who has
guardianship of his nephew becomes his wife!
Leon thinks Helen's experienced—until their
wedding night reveals otherwise....

ARISTIDES'
CONVENIENT WIFE

by Jacqueline Baird

Book #2630

Coming in May 2007.

www.eHarlequin.com

HPAMM0507

Silhouette®
Desire

Introducing talented new author

TESSA RADLEY

*making her Silhouette Desire debut
this April with*

BLACK WIDOW BRIDE

Book #1794
Available in April 2007.

Wealthy Damon Asteriades had no choice but to
force Rebecca Grainger back to his family's estate—
despite his vow to keep away from her seductive
charms. But being so close to the woman society once
dubbed the Black Widow Bride had him aching to
claim her as his own...at any cost.

On sale April from Silhouette Desire!

**Available wherever books are sold,
including most bookstores, supermarkets,
discount stores and drugstores.**

Visit Silhouette Books at www.eHarlequin.com SDBWB0407

BRIDES OF CONVENIENCE

**Forced into marriage—
by a millionaire!**

Read these four wedding stories
in this new collection by your
favorite authors, available in
Promotional Presents May 2007:

THE LAWYER'S CONTRACT MARRIAGE
by Amanda Browning

A CONVENIENT WIFE
by Sara Wood

THE ITALIAN'S VIRGIN BRIDE
by Trish Morey

THE MEDITERRANEAN HUSBAND
by Catherine Spencer

Available for the first time at retail outlets this May!

www.eHarlequin.com

HPP0507

REQUEST YOUR FREE BOOKS!

HARLEQUIN® *Presents*®

2 FREE NOVELS
PLUS 2
FREE GIFTS!

PASSION GUARANTEED SEDUCTION

YES! Please send me 2 FREE Harlequin Presents® novels and my 2 FREE gifts. After receiving them, if I don't wish to receive any more books, I can return the shipping statement marked "cancel." If I don't cancel, I will receive 6 brand-new novels every month and be billed just $3.80 per book in the U.S., or $4.47 per book in Canada, plus 25¢ shipping and handling per book and applicable taxes, if any*. That's a savings of close to 15% off the cover price! I understand that accepting the 2 free books and gifts places me under no obligation to buy anything. I can always return a shipment and cancel at any time. Even if I never buy another book from Harlequin, the two free books and gifts are mine to keep forever.

106 HDN EEXK 306 HDN EEXV

Name	(PLEASE PRINT)	
Address		Apt. #
City	State/Prov.	Zip/Postal Code

Signature (if under 18, a parent or guardian must sign)

Mail to the **Harlequin Reader Service®**:
IN U.S.A.: P.O. Box 1867, Buffalo, NY 14240-1867
IN CANADA: P.O. Box 609, Fort Erie, Ontario L2A 5X3

Not valid to current Harlequin Presents subscribers.

Want to try two free books from another line?
Call 1-800-873-8635 or visit www.morefreebooks.com.

* Terms and prices subject to change without notice. NY residents add applicable sales tax. Canadian residents will be charged applicable provincial taxes and GST. This offer is limited to one order per household. All orders subject to approval. Credit or debit balances in a customer's account(s) may be offset by any other outstanding balance owed by or to the customer. Please allow 4 to 6 weeks for delivery.

Your Privacy: Harlequin is committed to protecting your privacy. Our Privacy Policy is available online at www.eHarlequin.com or upon request from the Reader Service. From time to time we make our lists of customers available to reputable firms who may have a product or service of interest to you. If you would prefer we not share your name and address, please check here. ☐

HP07

From the magnificent Blue Palace to the wild
plains of the desert, be swept away as three
sheikh princes find their brides.

When English girl Sorrel announces she wishes to
explore the pleasures of the West, Sheikh Malik
must take action—if she wants to learn the ways
of seduction, he will be the one to teach her....

THE DESERT KING'S
VIRGIN BRIDE

by Sharon Kendrick

Book #2628

Coming in May 2007.

Men who can't be tamed...or so they think!

Damien Wynter is as handsome and arrogant as sin.
He will lead jilted Sydney heiress Charlotte to the altar and
then make her pregnant—and to hell with the scandal!

If you love *Ruthless* men, look out for

THE BILLIONAIRE'S
SCANDALOUS MARRIAGE
by Emma Darcy

Book #2627

Coming in May 2007.

Wined, dined and swept away by a British billionaire!

Don't be late!

**He's suave and sophisticated.
He's undeniably charming.
And above all, he treats her like a lady.**

But don't be fooled....

**Beneath the tux, there's a primal passionate lover
who's determined to make her his!**

Gabriella is in love with wealthy Rufus Gresham,
but he believes she's a gold digger.
Then they are forced to marry.... Will Rufus use
this as an excuse to get Gabriella in his bed?

Another British billionaire is coming your way in May 2007.

WIFE BY CONTRACT, MISTRESS BY DEMAND
by Carole Mortimer

Book #2633

www.eHarlequin.com   HPDAE0507